THE NINE-CHAMBERED HEART

Janice Pariat's debut collection of short stories, *Boats on Land* (2012), won her the Sahitya Akademi Young Writer Award 2013 and a Crossword Book Award for Fiction. Her first novel, *Seahorse*, was published in 2014 and was shortlisted for The Hindu Prize for Literature 2015. She has lived in London and Turin and is currently based in New Delhi.

Also by Janice Pariat

Boats on Land: A Collection of Short Stories
Seahorse: A Novel

The Nine-Chambered Heart

Janice Pariat

THE BOROUGH PRESS

The Borough Press
An imprint of HarperCollins *Publishers*
1 London Bridge Street
London SE1 9GF

www.harpercollins.co.uk

First published in Great Britain by HarperCollins *Publishers* 2018
1

A catalogue record for this book
is available from the British Library

ISBN: 978-0-00-827254-8

This novel is entirely a work of fiction.
The names, characters and incidents portrayed in it are the work of the
author's imagination. Any resemblances to actual persons, living or dead,
events or localities is entirely coincidental.

Set in 10.5/15 pts Scala FF
by SÜRYA, New Delhi

Printed and bound in Great Britain by
CPI Group (UK) Ltd, Croydon, CR0 4YY

MIX
Paper from
responsible sources
FSC® C007454

This book is produced from independently certified FSC™ paper
to ensure responsible forest management.

Find out more about HarperCollins and the environment at
www.harpercollins.co.uk/green

For the one who stayed the night

It is easy to love.
– Anaïs Nin

THE SAINT

THE BUTCHER

THE CARETAKER

THE UNDERTAKER

THE PROFESSOR

THE FLORIST

THE CRUSADER

THE LIGHTHOUSE KEEPER

THE SAILOR

THE SAINT

YOU ARE TWELVE, and you loathe me.

In my class, you refuse to paint, because you think your pictures are ugly. And I try and tell you, like every good teacher must, regardless of whether I believe it or not, that you'll improve with practice. You disagree. It infuriates you that there's something you can't immediately do, like a maths sum, or a science experiment. This is art, I tell you, but I can see you're a scientific artist. If there is such a thing.

The other children huddle around tables, painting and sketching in wild abandon. A few are truly accomplished. You are not one of them. Their hands move instinctively across canvas and paper, guided by some unseen spirit. Although I have a sorrowful feeling that this is the only time in their lives they will 'do' art. And that they will grow up and plunge into vocations that do not call for beauty.

Almost a year ago, on my first day here, in this small school, in this small town in the east of the country, I assigned the class to paint a tree.

'What kind of tree?' you asked.

'Any kind,' I replied.

'But there are so many kinds of trees...'

'I'm happy with any.'

That did not please you. And while you sat there undecided, the others dipped and dabbed, and I could tell that when you eventually tried, you were ashamed, even a little humiliated, that your tree looked like a green Popsicle on a stick. I made the mistake of coming round to your side of the table, and praising the girl to your right.

'Look... how she's allowed some sky to filter through the branches... That's how it is, isn't it? A tree is patchy. There are gaps between the leaves...'

You stared at me with something close to hatred.

It's a look I grew accustomed to those first few months. Everything I said, whether to you or another student, seemed incendiary. You didn't commit any overt misdemeanours, nothing I could throw you out of class or send you marching off to the headmaster for, which perhaps would have made it easier. Instead, it was a simmering, furtive mutiny. You did the barest minimum of work. Spending most of class time staring listlessly, excusing yourself to use the loo and not returning until just before the bell. You wouldn't care to

participate or answer questions, and anything I asked directly was met with a moody 'I don't know'.

In this way, we ploughed on through the year.

And even today, I get the same look of loathing. We're painting a snowy landscape in class, and I glance at the picture you've made, and say sharply, 'Have you ever seen pure white in nature?'

You frown. 'What do you mean?'

'I mean... snow is not white *white*, is it? There are shades of blue, and grey, and pink and yellow and purple even... the white wouldn't show if it were only white.'

And then I make the biggest mistake of all. I touch up your painting. I dip the paintbrush in a bit of blue, black, and water, and spread it over your landscape.

A touch here, a stroke there. I have improved the picture but lost you.

From now on, you refuse to pick up a brush. Even on threat of punishment and failure.

You are the most stubborn child I know, and make me long for the days of corporal punishment.

Later, when I ask the class to hand in their assignments for grades, you submit a blank page.

'What is this?' I ask crossly.

'White birds flying through white clouds.'

I give you an F. Then change it to a C. Rather than you failing, I have a feeling I've failed you.

We move on to other things, but you're spectacularly unskilled at each. Your still life sketches are weak, your charcoals messy. I cannot allow you to touch oils because they're expensive and I've been instructed to save them for the 'best' students in class. You're mystified by acrylics, using them like watercolours, but they dry too fast and leave hard blotches of colour in the wrong places.

Maybe later, when I've been teaching for years, I'll know how to deal with students like you. For now, I'm clueless.

I feel I've tried it all: threat, coercion, indifference, patience. I've spoken to your other teachers, and they can't understand it either. You're quiet and good in all their classes. Slightly scornful of chemistry, fond of literature, biology and history, and you're intuitively skilled at maths. But about that I'm not surprised.

I really do feel I've lost you, until one day I ask if you'd like to play with paper.

'And do what?' You sound scornful of this too.

'Well, we can make shapes for starters...'

You seem thoroughly unimpressed.

'Have you heard of origami?'

Tentatively, you shake your head.

How much you must hate admitting not knowing something. I'm almost gleeful.

I hand you sheets of paper and a beginner's How-To manual. I have a feeling you'd prefer this to taking instructions from me. You examine the pages, pick a pattern, lost in concentration. It's remarkable. You're marvellous at it. From your fingertips spring cranes and boxes, frogs and butterflies, crabs and flowers. Neat and intricate, the lines pressed and folded with industrious care and precision. They are exercises in exactitude. Each the same size and shape as the other. You sit in the corner of the classroom, patiently creasing, folding and lining them all up when they're done. I want to tell you they're beautiful, but I worry this might dissuade you instead, so I watch and do not offer praise.

After this, there's a sea change.

You are the first to enter class, and the last to leave.

Your eyes follow me around, while I'm moving from one cluster of students to another and when someone walks up to my desk for help. You linger at the end, showing me all you've made that day, eager, if I'm not mistaken, for my approval.

At first, I'm not quite sure how to respond. Do I appear pleased? Do I ignore you now, in return? I think in my confusion, I do a bit of both, but this doesn't deter you. If anything, it seems to make you even more determined. You catch me in corridors, and in the library, sometimes on the lawn, and initiate the most sweetly mundane conversation. We talk of the weather, and lunch, and whether I like cats or dogs.

'Dogs,' I say.

'Cats,' you say.

And everything I answer is followed by 'why?'

Why do I prefer peas to potatoes? Why would I like to own a bicycle rather than a car? Why dogs? Why am I vegetarian? Why do I like dark chocolate? Why do I read poetry? When I turn the questions back at you, I find you pleasingly impulsive. You don't take your time. You like beetroot for its colour. Cats for their eyes. White chocolate because it's not quite chocolate. Poetry befuddles you. You reply from your gut. Everything, at this age, is instinct.

You show me test papers and essays, work you've been merited on. I praise you like I think a parent would. You aren't that fond of sports, you tell me. Even though you're made to run and throw and participate. You're fond of music, but have no inclination to play an instrument. 'I like to sing,' you tell me shyly.

'Sing me something.'

'Just like that?'

'Just like that.'

We're outside, walking down a path in the school grounds.

'What would you like me to sing?'

'Anything.'

You take a moment to choose, and start singing. So softly, I must lean in to listen. It's an old song from the '70s. I wonder how you know it. Maybe your parents play it at

~ 8 ~

home, and you've grown up listening to it. It's a song about a man making a phone call to somebody he loved, and who left him. It's sweet and silly, and incongruous, coming from you, but you sing it to the end, and I applaud.

Once, you hand me a flower, a full, heavy magnolia blossom. It had fallen to the ground in the rain, and now lay in my hand, wetly glistening. Creamy pink, deepening in colour at the centre, palest at its waxy petal edges. I slip it into a bottle filled with water, and carry it home with me at the end of the day. I am thrilled by your attention, and also disconcerted. It is intense, like walking out into noonday sunlight. I've never been at the receiving end of something like this. And then I tell myself you are a child, that you cannot know better. Your feelings will turn this way and that, flitting from thing to thing, person to person. Soon enough you will tire of this, and someone else will fascinate you. But it doesn't seem to wane, your affection, anytime soon.

I think perhaps it is better to push you away slightly, to be a little distant, less accessible. After all, we don't want you doing something wayward. So I'm polite but more reserved. I duck into rooms if I see you coming down the corridor. I tell you I'm busy when you chance upon me in the library. I walk out of school with my other colleagues. I sit on the lawn with a book, preoccupied. You seem puzzled, though undeterred. But the more you clamour for my attention, the less I give you any. It's a terrible dance, and I feel sick, but I don't know what else to do.

On some days, I find paper cranes on my table, sometimes, a dragonfly.

At first I would collect them, placing them on a shelf like a disorderly, inanimate zoo. Now I try telling you that you could take them home to your parents to surprise and please them instead, but you look at me in silence. When I persist, eventually you say you can't, and you walk away.

This disturbs me, but it isn't something I can ask you about directly. At least not now. We haven't built up that kind of trust. I wonder if we ever will. So I speak to the other teachers, the ones who have taught you longer, and ask if they know more about you and your life at home. There are several conjectures. Someone asks, aren't you an orphan? Or the child of a single parent? No, say the others, they don't think it's like that at all, but there is something slightly out of the ordinary with your circumstances at home. Then your maths teacher speaks up, saying if he isn't mistaken it's not that you've lost your parents but that they live elsewhere, and so your home, at least during the school term, is with your grandparents. Not that you've been abandoned, he adds hastily, but your father works in another state, one with few if any, well-regarded schools. My heart goes out to you and your paper companions.

From then on, I am kinder.

You aren't entirely unskilled at clay sculpture, but I'm more encouraging than I would have been.

'That's a fine cow,' I say.

You look at me doubtfully. 'It's meant to be a horse.'

Hastily, I give a talk on how art lies in the eye of the beholder.

'So it doesn't matter what I'm trying to do?' another student asks.

'It does. But you cannot control how others choose to see.'

You stay back in class, hanging around until the others leave. I wonder why. I don't think you're about to ask me about the subjectivity of interpretation. You shuffle up to my desk, papers and books in hand. Your hair, usually braided in plaits, has come undone, your ribbon trailing down your arm. You are twelve, but your limbs seem at odds with your age, like they will settle only a decade later. You will be tall and beautiful, I'm sure, even if now you're gangly and awkward and coltish. You glance at me, your eyes dark as paint.

'Have you always wanted to do this?'

I ask what you mean.

'This.' You gesture around the room.

I lean back in my chair. No one has asked me this. At least not here. I could tell you many things. That of course it was a dream to work with children, to teach them about beauty, and how to make beautiful things. But I decide to tell you the truth.

'No.'

You don't seem surprised.

I look down at my hands, hold them up in front of me. 'I wanted to be a pianist.'

'Did you go to a music school?'

I nod. I did, for many years. I even began performing recitals here and there. Not much scope in this small town that we live in, so I would also give lessons at people's homes, trying to save up to move to a big city.

'Then what happened?' Or in other words, get to the point, why was I here.

'I was in an accident... I hurt my hands.'

With the cold pragmatism of a child, you look at me and say, 'But you still paint.'

I tell you it is all I can do.

'Oh,' you say, and leave. Maybe there was no reason for me to have been honest. You're a child. With limited understanding. What had I been hoping for? Sympathy? Concern?

I am left alone in the room, feeling, for some reason, decidedly silly.

In the next class, you are missing. And the next.

And even though I try and feign indifference, I'm concerned. What's happened, I ask the others. What's happened to you? A bronchial infection, apparently. One accompanied by a cough and high fever. I wrestle with myself, wanting to send you 'get well' wishes, yet wishing

to keep a distance. I know your classmates have made cards for you, but I don't jointly sign any of them. I don't send enquiries from my side. In ten days you return, paler, wan, still coughing. You've lost weight. I make you a little clay flower, paint it red, and leave it at your corner. I do it for all my students who've been ill. You thank me at the end of class, and don't linger like you usually do. It leaves me, uncomfortably, wondering why.

I find you quieter than usual.

You have stopped with the paper animals and clay figures, and instead are painting sheet after sheet of paper in deep, unvarying blue. Then orange. Then green. I joke that you're an abstractionist, but you do not laugh.

One day, I catch you in the corridor and ask how you are.

You don't look at me when you say you are fine.

'I heard you've been unwell...'

'Better now, thank you.'

'Is anything the matter?' I can't help asking.

You shake your head, your eyes still fixed to the floor.

I want to say that you can tell me, that you have someone you can talk to. That I know you live in a house with two old people, that you might feel alone. But I don't. I give you a perfunctory pat on the shoulder, and you're on your way.

It's odd, but I miss you staying back in class, chatting in your sharp, inquisitive way. I miss your singing, your flowers, your incessant questions, your attentiveness to everything I

say, even the merest, most mundane instruction. I hope it might revive at the end of term. Especially when I make the announcement that we're to hold an exhibition of all we've made over the past year. Most of the students are excited, whispering to each other, debating which of their works they'd like to display. Some have much to choose from. You look as though you haven't even heard me.

I allow a few classes to pass before I ask you. That afternoon, you've lingered, unintentionally, because a sheaf of your painted papers fell to the floor, scattering like leaves.

'Have you thought about it...?'

You stare up at me. Startled.

'What you'd like to display... for the end-of-year exhibition...'

You still look blank. It's exasperating.

'Yes...'

'Oh good. And...?'

'I'm still thinking... I don't know...'

I begin to make a few suggestions, and then stop. What am I doing? This is undoubtedly the best way to get you to *not* participate. 'Well... let me know if you need any help...'

You nod, and shuffle out of the room.

One day, when I've given up on any hope of you returning to your old self, you stay back in class. I'm at my desk examining some paintings for our show.

'What happened?'

I look at you, puzzled.

You come closer, clutching your books to your chest. You've never really recovered your weight since your illness, and your cheeks remain pale and hollow.

'What do you mean?'

You gesture at the paintings.

'I'm trying to choose frames...' I begin.

'No,' you interrupt. 'I mean your hands. What happened?'

I think I understand, but I don't want to answer. You persist.

'You told me you had an accident... and you couldn't play the piano any more...'

'I can still play,' I say, and add, 'But only a little.'

You stay silent, waiting for me to explain.

I push the paintings aside. 'I got a job with a choir... wonderful bunch of young kids... voices like angels and all that. It wasn't...' I laugh. 'We played mostly hymns, but it paid well and helped supplement my music lessons...'

You haven't taken your eyes off me. I don't know where to look, at you, at my hands. I settle for the window, where the late afternoon sun is streaming through and falling in patterns on the floor.

'We were travelling... for a concert in a nearby town. All of us in a bus... it was raining... I must have dozed off... but I remember waking up to a lurch... a terrible crash... the

bus crumpling like tin... and the seat in front of us suddenly pinning us back. If I hadn't put my... put my arms between the boy next to me and the metal, I think he would've been crushed...'

'You saved his life?'

'That's the thing... I'd like to think I did... but I don't know.'

'Your bones were broken?'

I nod. Grateful in a way for your stoic lack of emotion. By now most adults would be voicing profuse commiseration, and I would never know what to say to their 'I'm sorry... I'm so sorry... that's just terrible... what a tragedy...' I'd usually end up awkwardly saying 'thank you' and resigning myself to silence.

'Broken in several places...' I hold up my left arm. 'There's a steel rod running through this one.'

'Do you beep at airport security?'

I laugh, you laugh, and suddenly the room fills with light.

'Does it hurt?'

'Sometimes.'

Then you ask me something else no one has asked me before.

'If you were in that bus, would you do it again? What you did.'

It takes me a moment to reply. 'I'd like to say yes... but in truth, I'm not sure.'

You don't seem disappointed. In fact, you nod briskly, as though this is a business conversation. I want to ask you several questions in turn, about you, your home. But this is akin to having a bird finally sit on your hands and peck at crumbs. Now is not the time to make sudden movements or loud noises and frighten it away.

As you walk out of the classroom, you turn back. 'You know,' you say, 'I think you would.'

Soon enough it's end of term, and we're setting up the exhibition hall. You haven't submitted anything. I'm disappointed, yes, but not immensely surprised. I can't even use the line I do with the other kids – 'Wouldn't you want your parents to see your work and be proud of you?' I'm not sure yours are coming. And I don't want to hazard saying 'grandparents' instead. I don't know why, but I feel it's a delicate situation. Or at least I treat it so.

While the work is being put up, you hang around.

Because I think you expect it, I don't ask you where your contribution is. I ask you what you think.

'About?'

'All this...' I gesture around the room, filling up with paintings, sketches, sculpture.

'I want to see what it looks like when it's finished.'

And I find it hard to get another word out of you. But I see that you watch carefully, where everything is being placed.

Right now I have no time to question why or wonder. This is my first event, it must be impressive, and it must somehow validate... something.

I leave late that evening, after all the children's artworks have been put up. It's looking, I think, quite lovely. What a pity you aren't part of it. I'm tempted to place some of the paper figures you've gifted me in a corner, but desist. This is your choice and I must respect it. You did not feel involved enough in this class to wish to participate.

The next day, I arrive early at school and head to the exhibition hall. But someone else has been there earlier. Or that's what the security guard tells me. 'One of your students,' he says. 'Said she had your permission... special permission... to place something in the room. She had a lot of stuff with her...'

'What do you mean?' Panic pricks my chest. 'Which student? What was she carrying?'

He shrugs. Clearly not comprehending why I would be worried. 'Scissors... paper... art stuff like that...'

'I didn't give anyone permission to do anything.'

Finally, he seems a touch concerned. 'You didn't?'

I shake my head.

He fumbles with the door, unlocking it and drawing it open. We make our way briskly down the corridor.

In my head, I imagine everything in ruins. Paintings ripped out of their frames, shredded and sliced to strips.

Canvas torn, sculpture thrown across the floor, smashed to pieces. I can barely conceal my anger. Who could have done this? And why? For a flickering moment I think of you, and force myself to discard the idea. I have no proof. And why would the first person I think of be you? Perhaps because of your sullenness, your plummeting moods, your aloofness. But you haven't been that way all the time. You've never struck me as vindictive. Still, who knows? Children can be strange creatures. I try to shake it out of my head before we enter the hall. The security guard and I are silent.

I step in and everything is in its place, just as we left it the previous evening. Nothing seems to have been touched or broken or moved.

'All okay?' asks the guard.

I nod.

'Well, that's a relief.'

And then I see it. What you'd come in for, earlier this morning.

At the door leading outside, on the other side of the room, a curtain of white.

I can't really tell what it is, fabric or ribbon, until I walk closer.

Paper cranes. String after string. I stir them gently, and they rustle against my hand. Pristine white. Neat and even. Made with industrious care.

They are a thousand, I am certain even without counting.

They say folding a thousand cranes will grant you a wish.
I wonder what it is you've wished for.
I hope so much it will come true.

THE BUTCHER

I LOVE YOU. I almost hit you.

You're lodged in a corner, screaming at me, and I raise my hand. I can still see your eyes widen, your mouth round into a silent 'O' as the words die in your throat from surprise. And fear.

The evening didn't start out this way. No, *we* didn't start out this way.

Years ago, I remember. I see you across a bonfire on New Year's Eve. All soft and glowing, lit by the light of the flames. I'm rolling a joint and you catch my eye. After that, millions of sideward glances, a small smile or two, laughter. A reshuffling of places as people stand to refill their drinks, use the loo, seek cigarettes and matches. At some point, we find ourselves seated next to each other. I pass you a joint and you take delicate puffs, most of the smoke escaping your mouth. I wish I could say something witty, or smart.

~ 23 ~

That I could quote a line from a book or something, so that whatever we might share after this, however extended or fleeting, would always have this beginning. Instead, when you hand the joint back, I hear myself say, 'Good stuff, no?'

And in an instant, everything becomes forgettable.

You're older.

I've just begun university and you're in your final year.

'Please don't ask "what next"...'

I was about to, but protest, saying I wasn't, and comment on the weather instead. Something truly meaningful about it being cold. You make no reply.

Fuck. It's some terribly banal conversation I'm attempting. But you make me nervous. Even if I've just met you, I feel I must appear more than I am, or have ever been. A better version of myself, shinier, somehow more brilliant. Much later, I will put it down to something simple. Awe. Like you're some rare bird visiting a garden. Stupid as it might sound, at the time it feels like a privilege, that you should choose me. I've never been gladder that I left home, a small town in the east of the country, and moved to the capital, the city without a river. I've always had a sense that everything beyond is so much larger, that it moves to crazy rhythms, and contains people like you. That night, I sit next to you, joint following joint, expanding my senses into the sky. This is what it was like, I think, for explorers, perched on the brink

of an expedition. You an undiscovered continent. A land that hasn't been charted. And in a way, for me, the world.

That night around the bonfire a discussion breaks out.

We're an odd group. All of us having headed out for the weekend to this hill station. Cheap. Good weed. Popular with backpackers. The place we're staying in has a terrace, and there we all congregate. Some foreigners, some locals, a large college bunch from the city. It isn't yet midnight, but late enough for a friendly buzz rising with the fumes of cheap alcohol. Small talk has been made, travel stories swapped. Time then for drunken philosophizing.

Someone asks, 'What would you do if it could be seen?'

'What?' I ask. I haven't been paying attention.

'Grief.'

I say I don't understand.

Future grief in the face of someone you've just met.

'What do you mean?'

'Grief that you will cause. Someone you will be with. If you could see it, would it deter you? Or would you be willing to take the risk, test the prophecy?'

I say I would.

A clash of opinions come flooding in. It's cruel. No, surely now that one is aware, it can be avoided. Yet, isn't that the thing about prophecies? They are self-fulfilling. The argument continues. I lose interest. You, I notice, remain quiet.

Later, I go back to the room of a French tourist. It isn't my first time. I'd slept with a girl in my hometown a few months before I left for the city. We had lain naked on the bed of a friend's ground-floor bedroom, and heard abuses hurled through the darkened window, along with the clatter of stones on the roof.

'What's happening?' she had asked in fright.

'Someone saw us,' I said. Probably our friend's nosy and deeply religious neighbours. 'Should we stop?' she asked.

'No.' I was almost in her. And when I pushed myself inside, I shuddered and was still in less than a minute. It isn't that quick with the French girl. She emits tiny, excitable squeals that distract me. It's cold. The bed a slab of ice. I'm clumsy. She likes biting, and I wince as she almost draws blood from my lip. I like her blonde hair though, and her shapely waist, her long legs that wind around me. Finally, I bury my face in her shoulder, above her small pear-like breasts, thrust hard and quick, and it's over soon enough. I'm thinking of you at the bonfire.

I don't meet you again until a month later. At a student party, back in the city without a river. One of those unwieldy gatherings that usually ends in a drunken brawl. I find you on the balcony, looking as though you're waiting for no one. This time, I think, I'll say something memorable.

'Where were you while we were getting high?'

For a moment you look confused, then you smile.

'I came back with another joint... and you were gone.'

'It was cold... I was sleepy.'

I light a cigarette and lean on the railing.

'Did you have a good time... that night?'

I nod, remembering, in a flash, the blonde girl. 'Would've been better if you were there...'

'I'm here now.'

'For how long?'

You glance at your almost empty plastic cup. 'As long as the alcohol lasts.'

'So that's ten more minutes, then.'

When you laugh, I want to kiss you.

It turns out you too are from my small town in the east of the country. But from a different, posher, neighbourhood. Also, you've lived here for quite a few years now. 'And maybe at some point, elsewhere,' you add. I have a feeling you might be more of a drifter than I am. For even though I want to get away, I know my roots. I drop you back to your flat that night on my motorbike. I drive slowly, because I want to reassure you that I'm a safe driver. Also, I want the ride to last. Your hands gripping my sides, the feel of your chest on my back.

When we arrive, I ask, 'I'll see you soon?'

You nod. Then, with a wave, you're gone.

I'm amazed by how we begin with so little, or no, conflict.

It's not what I have known.

I'm only twenty-two but life has been long.

I started out studying something my parents thought useful. Two semesters in biotechnology though, and I'd failed every exam, spent all the money I'd been given for the year, and switched courses. To the fury of my physician father, of course. But my mother, the gentler of the two, persuaded him to let me be. If it was visual studies I wanted to pursue, so be it.

I never told them that all I really wanted was to be a musician.

'You play well,' you tell me.

We are at a house party, sitting in the living room where I've found a guitar. 'Thanks,' I say. 'I taught myself.'

I don't tell you yet that my parents only sent my younger sister for piano lessons. That they thought, being a boy, I wouldn't – no, shouldn't – be interested in such frivolities.

You move closer. You're wearing a long woollen skirt, a frayed leather jacket, and a polo neck. Your hair is tied up, loosening around the edges.

'What would you like me to play?'

'Ooh, he's taking requests,' someone shouts from the other end of the room.

'Not from you, Bongo,' I shout back.

Since you say 'anything', I play the songs I know best. Some Marley and Led Zep, some Dylan and Clapton. You sing in snatches, in a soft, pleasant voice.

'Something by the Beatles?'

Suddenly, I feel like I have only one chance to pick the right song. That it will make all the difference. I run through the ones I know in my head. 'Come Together'. 'Penny Lane'. 'Yellow Submarine'. 'Eleanor Rigby'. They all somehow seem inappropriate, until I remember the one about a blackbird and broken wings. Sweetly complex melody, and sweetly simple lyrics. Turns out you know all the words. Verse after verse. The room falls silent, with only the guitar and your voice filling the air. I know, no matter what, that when I drop you home that night, we will kiss.

You live in a flat you share with two other girls. It's a nicer neighbourhood than the one I live in, with trees and wide roads. Your room, when I get to see it, has multicoloured curtains drawn over the windows, a low bed, a ragged carpet, and photographs pasted on the cupboard. You've twirled a scarf over a tall paper lamp. I like it better than the place I share with three boys, littered with used plates, discarded footwear and empty bottles. We are quite lucky, you say, when I first stay over, that the landlord doesn't live in the building, and so can't express his disapproval over these 'indiscretions'.

I'm taller than you but we fit on the bed, oddly sized between single and double, if I press my back against the wall. And if we don't move much.

We don't move much, but we talk. I like you because when I say, late one night, in the dark, that I want to start a band, you don't laugh.

Bolder, I make you listen to a song I recorded, secretly, in my room in my hometown. It's stark and sad, about a man who drinks in parking lots. I don't think it's very good now, but you listen intently, and say you think I've done well.

'But I can do better.' With you, I want to add, I feel I can always do better.

You, though, rarely talk about yourself. Only once you tell me about your parents, and how they always lived away from you because of your father's job.

'I'd tell people they were dead. That they died in a car crash.'

'Why?' I ask, bewildered. 'Why would you do that?'

Your voice is soft in the darkness. 'Because I was angry. They kept promising they'd come back for good, but they never did.'

Another night, after we've had more than a few beers each, you tell me that once, when your parents left after their yearly visit, you were so upset you fell ill with a fever that lingered for weeks.

'I was eleven... twelve... I couldn't understand why I was always left behind...'

Silently, I promise I'll never leave you.

But it's a promise I eventually find impossible to keep.

When summer comes around, we turn nocturnal.

We return from university to darkened houses, the sound of other people's power generators studding the air like quiet gunfire. It is impossible to sleep. The heat seeps out of floors and walls, out of every surface we touch. We throw down buckets of water, we soak the sheets, but the heat is insidious. So we drive out on my motorbike and head to the centre of the city, where the roads are wide and all the filthy rich sleep in their beds under the cool purr of air conditioners that never trip or turn off.

'Bastards,' we yell as we cross their gates, my motorbike roar shattering the silence. Then we stop at some patch of grass, with all the poor others who've found their way there in those restless, insomniac nights. Sometimes, we buy orange ice lollies from the man with the ice cream cart, and while I bite into mine whole, you suck at the juice until the ice turns white.

'You're a vampire.'

And you pretend to bite my neck, and I pin you to the grass, and I want to lift your dress.

We are wild children.

Once the summer cools, and the rains lighten in the north, we head to the hills. Our first trip away together. It is also the first time we have a terrible fight. The first of many.

To begin with, we miss our stop. We were meant to disembark at six in the morning, but we were fast asleep,

buried in our jackets and shawls on the cold hard seats. By the time we awake, we've overshot our destination by three hours and must make our way back on a rumbling local bus.

When we arrive at the town in the mountains, we disagree over where to stay.

'This is too fancy,' I hiss into your ear at the hotel that charges five hundred bucks a night.

'Where do you want to go then?'

'Somewhere else.' I don't add 'cheaper'.

'We've just spent twenty hours on the road and you want to walk around some more?'

'This is the first place we've looked at.'

And so we do, but everywhere else we look for cheaper, you detest. Too dirty. Too small. Damp walls. And so we end up back at the place where we started.

'I'll pay for both of us,' you declare.

And that annoys me even more. 'It's not about the fucking money,' I say. It is, but it also isn't, and I know you won't understand.

That evening, when an unquiet calm has settled, we head into town. Almost immediately, we're accosted by a sad, red-eyed rat of a peddler who walks next to me asking if I want some hash.

'Ignore him,' you say, but it's too late. I've already said, 'How much?' I couldn't help it. It's instinctive.

He names a price, insane as it is, and then won't leave us. You don't say a word but I can feel your anger, hot and

silent. When the rat pushes the hash into my jacket pocket and then pretends like I'm the one not paying up, I get really mad. I give him his thousand and then throw the stuff into the nearest dustbin.

'Okay I'm sorry, all right?' I offer, but you stay quiet.

We find our way to a rooftop restaurant where backpackers are sitting on cushions around the edges, drinking beer. The walls are graffitied, and lanterns dangle from bamboo poles. Our moods improve after some food. We start making conversation again. You dig your socked feet under my thigh to keep warm. I tuck a strand of hair behind your ear. Night falls thick and fast, and the mountains behind us disappear into darkness. The alcohol warms us. Someone passes us a joint. We sit closer. Then a guitar is brought out from downstairs.

'Who can play?' shouts the owner.

You pull up my hand.

And the night passes by in a blur of song and music, and faces and smoke. People gather around me, bottles in hand, glasses glinting like stars. My voice, and their voices, and ours, rise over the rooftops. There's a woman with long, dark blonde hair, wearing a Tibetan jacket, smiling at me. A boy with an earring passing me spliff after spliff. We sing endlessly. The songs we all somehow seem to know. It's one of those moments when you feel music will make everything all right, and the world isn't such a shitty place after all. If

we just keep singing, it will all stay the way it is, frozen in that moment.

The next day, you're gone.

I wake up alone in the hotel room. A crumpled, slovenly mess. The bed, not me. Although I don't feel well either. Across the sheet, emptiness, a pillow. I call out to you. Maybe you're in the loo. I call you again. I heave myself up and check, now stung by fear and worry. Your side of the bed looks slept in, I think. Anyway, how can one tell? I'm sure we came back together. Am I? Yes, I think we stumbled back together at dawn, me glowing in the aftermath of performance. For a real, live audience. I feel I've never played better, or more skilfully. I remembered lyrics, and manoeuvred my way through complicated chord progressions. When we reached our room, I groped you drunkenly, I remember, from happiness, lifting your sweater, moving my hands over your breasts, kissing your neck. I think you pushed me away. I must've tried again before slumping asleep.

Now, in the late morning, it comes back to me in flashes.

I'm not sure where to start, but I head out. The guy at the reception is clueless when I ask if he's seen you. The town is small, but feels endless when I step outside. I walk down to the main road, the one flanked by matchbox clothes stalls, still-closed restaurants, and women in shawls selling steaming dumplings. Maybe you were hungry and came

looking for food. Maybe I'll find you standing by one of these makeshift street-food vendors, eating momos. 'Here,' you'll say, holding one out to me. Your eyes, as usual, will be rimmed by the kohl you didn't clean off, your hair bundled untidily into a bun. Suddenly, your absence feels like a stab in my stomach. I must find you. Somehow my feet make their way to where we were last night. Up the stairs, to the rooftop restaurant, which is all but deserted apart from a group of trekkers eating breakfast. Oddly, I can't remember where you were while I was playing the guitar. Next to me, of course. Or was that the lady with the dark blonde hair and the Tibetan jacket? She was very friendly. At one point, hadn't she asked me to show her how to strum?

In half an hour, I feel I've exhausted all possibilities and walked that main road to death. I'm beginning to waver now, between anger and fear. Why the fuck are you doing this? What if something happened to you? I'm hungry and hung-over, and the weed has left a bitter, burnt taste in my mouth. I wolf down a plate of dumplings and then feel guilty. I shouldn't waste any time. I must find you. When I think I've run out of options, I walk down the road that takes us out of town, towards the highway. Here too are shops and a sprinkling of small eating joints. I pass one that's placed higher than the rest, on a raised platform, with outdoor tables and chairs.

Sun Moon Café it's called, and I think that's the kind of place you would like.

There's someone sitting outside, reading. It looks like you. It *is* you.

I yelp in relief. You look up at me, and turn back to your book. 'What the fuck,' I mutter, as I run up the steps.

'Where were you?' I say. I realise it's a stupid question even before you reply.

'Here.'

'Why did you leave like that?'

You shrug.

'I was worried, man.'

I hear you mutter something.

'Is this about last night?'

'What do you think?'

I hate it when you do this. Turn the question back at me. I'm only trying to figure out what the fucking matter is. I care enough to do this. Why isn't that good enough? I take a deep breath, trying to keep the glimmer of anger at bay.

'Something about last night upset you... except I don't remember much...'

You snort, in laughter, disdain.

'What, man?'

'So convenient.'

'We drank a lot...'

'Yes, we did. Except that still didn't make me throw my arms around some blonde stranger.'

'I was showing her how to strum!'

'Oh, is that what you call it, you wannabe rock star?'

I am struck, at this moment, by how precisely we know how to hurt the ones we love.

It doesn't go on for long, this argument. Mostly because I think we're exhausted, or at least I am. And also, no matter what, I'm relieved to have found you.

We return to the city without a river. Something has changed. We are closer, yet further apart. That doesn't make sense, but it does. Our quarrel revealed how much we care for each other, but it wounded deep. Here I am, a fucking contradictory wreck. I look to you to feel good, but I realise that if I give someone that power, they can also make me feel like shit about myself. You never say 'wannabe rock star' again, although other hurtful things are hurled around the room. We are knife throwers in a circus. Bring on the clowns, and the little dog in a big bow that jumps through hoops. Sometimes, I think I am all of them rolled into one.

It is worse because I have never seen you this way. Suddenly restless and complaining all the time about the city, your flatmates, your university. You feel it's all a waste.

'This is not what I'm meant to do,' you say. And when I ask what it is that you do want, you don't reply. You don't know, and I think that's what annoys you. I don't know when you'll snap next and for what reason.

The other night, I asked if I could borrow a couple of plates from you for a shoot in college. Some video project for class.

'No.'

'It's just some plates, man.'

'No,' you shouted back, your eyes filling with tears. 'You'll break them.'

'It's just a fucking shoot,' I yelled back and left, slamming the door behind me. By the time I returned, you were in bed, the lights were off. I don't know if you were asleep, but you didn't speak.

One evening, we watch a movie. Something that had been screened in class that I wanted to share with you. We do this often. You recommend books, that I admittedly don't read, and I bring back films in my hard drive, filched from friends at university. Within the first five minutes, barely after the opening credits, we are arguing. A shot of a woman lying on a bed in her underwear, from behind, and I remark on the camera's 'male gaze'. It's something our professor had mentioned.

You roll your eyes.

'What?'

'The movie's directed by a woman... so perhaps this is somewhat subversive.'

We don't finish watching the film.

The night I almost hit you, we are headed to a blues bar hosting a live act. These are my favourite evenings in the city. Back home, the streets fold into themselves by six. Here,

nothing begins until late. Even if I'm not performing, nothing makes me happier than being someplace where someone is. You seem all right when we leave. We get on my bike and head south. You seem all right even when we get there. When we climb the stairs and step into a dimly lit room. There's the stage. The audience, with drinks in hand. The band is setting up. Sound check. The first number. They're good. Not brilliant, but I don't really care. You seem all right even when you meet a few people you know, and make conversation. When you sip your drink, and bob your head to the music.

See, that's the thing, I can't tell the moment when you're not all right. It's a switch that takes seconds.

Suddenly, you're tugging at my sleeve saying you want to leave.

'Why?'

'I want to go...'

'But they've just started.'

'This place is awful...'

'It's fine... I want to stay...'

'And I don't want to.'

It carries on like this, and the band's really getting into it now. Something strong and bluesy bursts into the air. I'm beginning to get annoyed.

'You stay,' you say, 'I'll go.'

'No,' I shout over the music. 'We came together, we leave together.'

'That's ridiculous...' you begin to say when I walk out. I only know you're following when I hear your feet clatter behind me on the stairs. We step out into the evening. You're saying something, but I can't hear you through the throb of my anger. I feel something strike me on the side of my head.

'What the fuck?' I roar, turning. You've flung a magazine at me. For a second, I pause to wonder where you got it from. Strange, isn't it, the things that occupy us even at moments like these?

Back at your flat, the argument continues.

'It wasn't a big deal,' you yell. 'You could've stayed... I could've left.'

'We went together, we leave together,' I shout back. I don't know why, but I'm hung up on this line. It's become precious to me, this idea. We are loud, and I'm sure people outside, downstairs, upstairs can hear us. I don't give a shit. We shout at each other.

'You threw that magazine at me...'

'Because you wouldn't stop and listen.' Your voice is shrill and piercing. I cannot bear it.

It seems like you're raising your hand against me. So I raise my hand too. Your eyes widen, your mouth rounds into a silent 'O' as the words die in your throat from surprise. And fear.

'Look what you made me do,' I shout. 'Look what you made me do.' I am the worst, most vile version of

myself. I am crumbling like a pile of garbage. I am a pile of garbage.

With you, I am highest, and lowest.

It isn't this, though, that breaks us up.

We continue for weeks, months. Over a year. Two. At a wedding you get pissed off because I'm chatting for too long, you say, with some other woman. Another time, you find an email exchange on my laptop between some girl and me, entirely innocent in content, but then why haven't I told you about her? Back home, I've seen butchers dice meat, and sometimes pieces string together because the cut isn't clean. We hold on like that too. Unhappy together, but what if we're unhappier apart? I think, at times, we would be. Because, no matter what, we do have fun. We sing a lot, with me on the guitar. A bottle of whisky. You dancing on the bed. We still drive around the city at night, and eat ice cream, and go to gigs.

But eventually, all this is not enough.

One evening, after a fight about I don't even remember what, I storm out of your flat and go to my friend's house to spend the night. We drink. There's meat being cooked. We sample some weed from the hills. Some time just before dawn, when I'm lying awake in an unfamiliar room, I send you a text. It's the coward's way out, I know, but maybe that's all I am.

I say I can't do this any more. That it's over.

You don't reply. Not then. Maybe you never will.

I stare at the screen. The light fades, and it finally dies into darkness.

THE CARETAKER

You're half my age, maybe younger, but I see you and I want you.

I've felt it before, this kind of want. It's raw and easy, and instantly recognizable, like hunger, and as uncomplicated – mouth to gut. With you, though, I'm afraid.

At this time of night, it might be the alcohol. How much have I had to drink? Always one too many. In my head, that familiar lightness, and the hall in which this gathering is taking place has taken on a certain hazy glow.

I see you clearly as you step into the room. You stand uncertainly for a moment, glance about you, and walk across to where the door opens towards a small lawn. You stop just beyond the glow of the wood burner. Why would you do that? It's December, and cold, and your dress – if that's what it can be called – won't do much to keep you warm. It's a

cross between kimono and lab coat, with sleeves that swirl like windmills. On my wife it would look like an eccentric bathrobe, but you it suits, that touch of the dramatic. You seem to be a woman to whom something is always about to happen.

I watch you from a distance; sip my whisky – both in unhurried pleasure. I am called to your face. That nose, that sweep of brow, something about your chin. Your hair is long, but swept deliciously away from your neck, piled on top. You are pleasingly – not conspicuously – tall. As a child you must have been awkward, gangly, I'm certain of it, but not now, not any more. And if I were a poet I'd find a way to describe your body as it deserves to be. All that comes to mind is a tree, a cypress, whose leaves shimmer in the sunlight.

I watch as you gaze into the wood burner, your face indecipherable. Are you thoughtful? Bored? Dulled by your surroundings? Quietly contemplating setting the place on fire? For the moment, nobody joins you; you stand alone while the people around you ebb and flow. It doesn't seem like you know anyone and no one else knows you. In which case, why are you here? I edge closer, and am accosted by acquaintances. Hard not to run into somebody I don't know. It's a large gathering, teeming with fat journalists and faded writers. All right, that's unfair and untrue. It's a nicely cultured lot; some who've known each other for years, and pride themselves on their perspicacious social contacts

and good intentions. This is some book launch or the other, I'm not sure. More like an excuse for all of us to gather and drink middlingly expensive alcohol, eye each other's partners, check out the new youngsters on the scene. You can spot them a mile away. They're eager, and they smile a lot, and say things like, 'Yes, I'm a poet.'

Perhaps you're a friend of one of these youngsters, for somehow, you aren't quite... indigenous. You seem – and I'm not prone to using the word – unreal. Suddenly, I grow afraid you'll walk into the shadowy edges of the lawn and I'll lose you. If I don't speak to you now, you'll step away from the fire and disappear.

So I walk up and ask why you don't stand closer to the burner.

'It's pointless.'

'To keep yourself from freezing to death?'

'Perhaps. Only it's much worse to warm just your hands, don't you think? Or your – back.' I think you almost said 'ass', but maybe I seem dignified (read 'old'), and you haven't drunk enough wine yet. Besides, for now, we're strangers.

'I'd rather be cold all over.'

'Or warm all over.'

Did that sound cheap? I took care to say 'warm' instead of 'hot'.

You turn to me.

Your eyes fall on my neck. I'm certain you're thinking, 'Oh god, he wears cravats.' I've always felt they suit me; that a tie is a touch too plebeian. Although maybe to you, it makes me look ancient. I'm barely past fifty, but at twenty-something, that must seem light years away.

'Do I know you?' you say, fixing your gaze on me.

I shake my head, almost imperceptibly. Suddenly, I imagine slipping a hand around your waist, preferably naked. It's most inappropriate.

'Is that a dress?' I hear myself utter foolishly.

I'm not usually like this; it's rather easy, this well-rehearsed routine, except perhaps the others hadn't been so young or so disconcerting.

'What I mean is... it's a striking outfit.'

'Thanks.' You lift a hand and a sleeve falls open like a wave.

'Where do you live?' I ask.

'There.' In a flat you share with two girls.

'What do you do?'

'Not much.'

I like you. I really like you.

I ask if you've ever bothered to do boring things... like go to university.

You did, and you're done. It's been several years. And if I really want to know, you add, you've just quit your first job. Some stint at a publishing house.

'What do you want to do now?' As soon as I ask this, I feel as though I've fallen, even further, in your estimation.

But your reply comes swift and simple: 'I don't know.'

I can't help but laugh. 'Forgive me,' I say, 'but I haven't heard that in a long while. It's the privilege of youth, the envy of the old.'

'You're not – old.'

I raise my glass – 'You're not unkind' – and walk away.

I spend the rest of the evening hoping it's worked.

That instead of lingering, as others might have done, to extend the conversation, it was cleverer to retreat, to watch if you search for my face across the room, if you cast glances as we pass. Only towards the end of the evening will I seek you out again, I decide – I'll appear casually beside you, as though from nowhere. Holding my glass delicately forward. (I fancy I have what are called pianist's fingers. Don't they hint at skill, and artistry? A certain poetic sensitivity?)

Instead, you find me.

'I meant it, you know.'

'Meant what?'

'That you're not old.'

'It helps not to be reminded.'

You flush fiercely, and say sorry.

'I was joking...'

'No, I shouldn't have.'

Over the months, I will grow to learn this about you: that you can be oddly, effusively apologetic to strangers. When I finally manage to convince you otherwise, I offer to drop you home. 'It's on my way...' I throw in, 'And this will prove I have no hard feelings.'

In the car we are silent, listening to the gentle drone of the engine. Lights glint off the windscreen like meteor showers. The city is bathed in the grey haze and desolation of winter. An airplane makes its solitary way across the sky.

'When will I see you again?' I ask.

Next year, at the same party.

'Well, that's a relief.'

You laugh.

I long to reach across and kiss you, and press my tongue into your mouth.

It's a mystery what I'll find there, even for someone who's lived this long and feels like they've seen all there is to see of corporeal life.

We've almost arrived, so I persist, gently. Lunch? Drinks?

When you hesitate, I imagine I'll have to explain.

There's no wedding ring. I took it off a long time ago. It didn't fit any more, and I was meant to get it recalibrated, but I never got round to it. You're so young, though, what would I say? It had been difficult, sometimes, with the others, when it was brought up, the subject of my wife. Did I love

her? Was it one of those marriages that had dissolved into indifference? Perhaps, but I'd never leave her. We didn't occupy separate bedrooms – nothing as clichéd as that – but we lived cosmically separate lives. She ran a school. I ran a magazine. It had been that way a long while. Some lovers left, bereft. Some stayed longer, because I was their secret too.

We come to a stop in front of your gate.

'It's somewhat complicated, isn't it?' I say.

'Why?' You have a way of saying this word that demands honesty.

'Because I'm so much older... and the whole marriage thing...' I'm fumbling now, out of nervousness.

'I don't care about you being older. But what marriage thing?'

'I'm married.' I wait for you to step out of the car, angry, disgusted.

Instead you lean towards me, and I kiss you, quickly, as though I'm coming up for air.

We start meeting in my spare apartment in the city, a fortnight later.

The tenants have left, and I've found no one else to rent it out to yet.

'I think I'll keep it just for us,' I tell you. I like watching you in the empty rooms, bare as they are, feline in your small, quiet movements. You fit into its corners and niches,

pad across the floor barefoot, lie on the terrace in the winter sun. It becomes your space even though you add nothing more to it than your presence. Sometimes flowers, leaves that have fallen on the road and you've picked up on your way. And cats, but that isn't until later.

The first time we go out together, for a drink at a bar, low-lit and discreet, I ask why you agreed to see me. You sip your red wine – I ordered you a bottle of medium-bodied Nero d'Avola – and look me in the face. 'Curiosity.'

I like you. I really do.

Beneath the softness, there's grit. It shows in your mouth, when you don't wish to reply, in the tilt of your head. Even in how much you can drink. I am amazed that you keep up with me, glass for glass. Then even more, when I'm done.

It must be youth. They don't know it, but the young drink to die. Alongside raging life runs an urge to extinguish themselves. It has to be. There's no other explanation for this hedonism.

That night, I half carry you home, into your room.

'Wow, you're so cool,' remarks one of your flatmates. Only later do I realise she must've thought I was your father.

The second time we meet, I take you to see some art.

Folk art as they call it in these circles. What I've been collecting these past few years, my newest fixation. (Although that might be you.) I take you to the agent's house, in a quiet

leafy colony, and you saunter in after me like you've done this a hundred times before. You stop at each painting that accompanies us down the stairs to the basement. For all your nonchalance, you are mesmerised by two peacocks, feathers unfurled, dancing.

'Beautiful,' you say, 'like pointillism.'

I'm delighted.

In the 'gallery', we wander around; I'm followed by an eager assistant, you on your own. I'd like to buy you a painting, of course. Because it'll impress you I'm sure, and also because I cannot believe you are here with me, by my side.

When I suggest it, though, you balk. No, you say, pick something up for yourself. These are expensive, I cannot accept. I don't listen to you. I choose a tiger, it's red and black and crouching, like love. You walk to the car with it, in a daze.

As we're driving back, you sit quietly, your elbow on the open window, until it grows too cold and you roll it up, and place your hands neatly on your lap. It's an oddly touching gesture. I feel an overwhelming urge to draw you close.

I hold your hand, and you let me.

The third time we meet, I take you back to the apartment, after a dinner of artichokes, and gnocchi made with baby spinach, and soft-shell crabs. Such a treat. For the city without a river is also a city without the sea. We linger over

our drinks. I sense you are in an expansive mood, that the evening will not end in a chaste farewell.

Nevertheless, in the car, I ask if you'd like to be dropped home.

'No.'

We kiss as soon as we walk in through the door of the apartment, in a room where the pieces of furniture, covered in sheets, are ghosts. You sigh as we part, your face now framed by hair that has tumbled – I hadn't noticed when – over your shoulders. I place my hands on your waist. This is what it must be like, I think, to hold a cluster of river reeds. That night, we don't even make it to the room with the bed. We move on to the couch, wide and roomy, and I undress you in the dark. The only glow comes from an outside street light, but it's enough for me to see the curve of your shoulders and breasts, the line of your neck when you lift your head in pleasure, the swell of your thighs. Your mouth is soft and responsive. It takes me by surprise. With me, you're friendly but guarded, yet your kisses are eager. I will remember you by this, always, that you are immensely giving. Here is all of me, your mouth seems to say, I do not hide myself.

Over the next few months, in between work meetings, I head to the apartment with the eagerness and elation of a teenager. You have the extra key, and often I find you there, sitting by one of the wall-length windows. We are on the second

floor, and all around us are trees. You said once that it was like being in a tree house and I can see why you'd like that; secret and removed from the world. Sometimes, I bring you treats. Fat oranges, crunchy pistachios, foreign genmaicha, or mille-feuille from a nearby bakery. I watch you eat, juice running down your chin, pastry flaking into your hand. Then I kiss you, and taste the saltiness and the sweet.

One hot, clammy afternoon, the windows curtained over by sheets, we lie on the bed, the room still and silent. I run my fingers down your back, the curve of it a young dove, your skin like feathers.

'Was it good?' I ask. I always ask, because I'm uncertain of myself, at this age, pleasing you.

You nod but do not expand, and I worry. Maybe it's my stomach, no longer as taut as I like to remember it, or my skin, wrinkling now as fast as raisins.

'When was your first time?' I ask before I can stop myself. I'm quite certain it isn't me, but somehow I wish it so.

You look me in the face.

I'm a moon, one half dark, the other lit by late afternoon sun.

You say you lost your virginity when you were nine.

I've heard these stories before; I try not to flinch.

'To a kitchen stool.'

You shouldn't take me for an idiot, I say, half laughing.

You prop yourself up on your elbows. 'But I'm not. It's the truth.'

It happened at dinner, you explain. You stood for a second helping, slipped, and the wooden edge rammed between your legs.

Your grandmother asked if you were all right, and you nodded, despite desperate pain. Later, you discovered your panties spotted scarlet. You hid in the bathroom all night; your grandparents outside the door, wild with worry.

I want to ask why you hardly, if ever, mention your parents, but perhaps now is not the time.

Instead I turn towards you, my face now fully in darkness.

'I could've died.'

'No, my silly one.' I stroke the smoothness of your cheek, the edges of your mouth, plump as fruit. Youth shimmering in sunlight. 'You will live forever.'

A week later, you bring the cats.

A pale ginger with eyes of warm amber, and a dark grey tiger-stripe with leaf-green eyes. You say you found them abandoned in a suitcase on the roadside. One of the girls with whom you share a flat is allergic to fur, and you have nowhere else to take them. You sit on the floor of the apartment, delighted, as they twirl about, twining around your ankles. I look on indulgently, as I would with a child. It's obvious, isn't it? You're young enough to be my daughter,

and it doesn't bother me, as much as makes me sometimes feel... fatherly towards you. It's strange; a daughter who is a lover, a lover who is a daughter. Whose breasts I suck on. Who moves on top of me, until she shudders and falls still. When I think of those things, I want to be in you. I wonder if you think of these things too, if, even for you, there is this oddness, a duality, secret and forbidden.

With the cats there, you stay over often, sometimes not returning to your own flat for days. I find a scattering of clothes in the cupboard, a toothbrush in the bathroom, sachets of shampoo, underwear drying on a line in the balcony. If I have an exhausting day at work, I'll get to the apartment, and we'll fall asleep on the bed, me holding you. Tight, tight. Because I know that, no matter how much I pretend, this will not, cannot, last. How could it? Me, old and attached, and you, as you are. You hold so much power in the palm of your hand. To walk away from this whenever you wish to. While I watch the bubble, and try so hard, on prayer alone, to keep it afloat.

All through that winter, I spend more time at the apartment than at home. It's cold in the city without a river. The days brief, the nights long. I bring along shawls and blankets, and we sit like children around the radiator, begging to be kept warm. I haven't, in a long while, known such... informality. You place your socked feet on my chest, between my legs,

on my back. While I do my best to undress you. I want not just to see your skin, but also to see whether you're intact, that the red beauty spot on your stomach, to the right side, is still there, that the one on your back, perfectly placed between your shoulder blades, hasn't shifted.

'It's freezing... what are you doing?' you'll ask, half laughing.

'Checking to see it's still you.'

And you'll be perfectly serious when you say, 'It's always me, you fool.'

How can anyone, I think, when I look down at you, lying under me, be so young?

No, that isn't the word. Youthful. Yes, youthful.

I suppose all I've noticed for years now is the human body in need of repair.

And you, you are perfect.

'Have you ever had an operation?' I ask you once.

You shake your head.

'Nothing? Not an appendectomy... tonsils?'

On your body, you say, not a stitch. You've scraped and hurt yourself, of course – on your palm, the scar from the tender bite of a pet dog, on your knee, an old wound that had become infected – but you've never been sliced by a scalpel. Never needed a threaded needle to hold flesh together. Silently, I hope you'll always stay this way, that you will remain intact.

One late afternoon, I find you wandering the street outside the apartment.

'China,' you say, 'China's gone.'

It takes me a moment to recollect that that's what you've named the ginger cat. (The tiger-stripe is India.) China clambered out to the balcony, spotted a bird and, unable to resist, leapt over the gap, fell to the balcony below, and dashed back out again on to the road in fright. You watched all this happen, helpless, and then rushed downstairs, calling out his name. When I find you, you've taken about twenty turns. China is still nowhere in sight. You aren't, as one might expect, apoplectic or hysterical, just deeply restless, unable to sit or stand still. I join you on the search. The two of us, to anyone watching, a father and daughter looking for our lost pet.

'He must be frightened and hiding,' I tell you. 'He'll come back later.'

But he doesn't, not that night or the next.

You leave the windows open; the apartment grows so cold we sleep with our jackets on. You put out plates of cat food on the balcony. 'But how will he climb up?' you agonise. And you want to take to the streets again. At first, I accompany you, exhausted, in the middle of the night. Then I try to make you see that there's no point. When China disappears, I realise there doesn't exist a body with no scars.

You stop going out to look for him but still keep the windows open. One morning, we wake to find India gone too. We'd left the bedroom door ajar, and he must've slipped out silently while we slept.

Then you weep, and don't stop. I've only seen such grief at funerals.

After that, I sense a retreat, as though you hold me responsible. I knew this was bound to happen, inevitable really, if you look at our situation. There is nothing I can do. There is nothing I can do enough.

'Why don't we get another cat?' I ask once, and you look at me as though I'm mad.

Before the disappearance of China and India, you would allow me to hold you when I spent the night. Now, there is a space between us on the bed, seldom bridged. When it is, I stroke your hair. Your sides, curving like hills. One night, I say that you will get over these abandonments, and then, because I feel compelled to be honest, that they may happen again.

'What do you mean?' you ask, your breath warm on my neck.

'Nothing.'

'Tell me.'

I regret it already. Who am I to warn you about these things? Can anyone ever be warned?

Just that, I reiterate, it might happen again, and that you'd be surprised at the lengths people would go to not to feel abandoned, or to abandon.

For a long while, you are silent. Then you say, 'I know.'

I want to laugh and say, aren't you too young to know, but there's a look on your face that stops me. I wait for you to speak, and you do, slowly, haltingly. 'I was with this guy once... and it was horrible at the end...'

'Why?'

'We fought... all the time... but we stayed together in spite of everything... probably because of this reason...'

'It's the hardest thing,' I say, 'to bring things to a close.'

'And you?'

We've never spoken of my marriage before.

'Even though you've been with other people, why do you still stay married?'

I have nothing to say but this pitiful thing. 'I'm not the kind of person to leave.'

And you lie back, staring at the white ceiling, and say you understand. I'm silent for a while, and then ask, 'Because you stayed with this... guy... even though you weren't happy?'

You nod. He wasn't either, you explain, but at least he knew when it was enough, when the unhappiness was too much, had gone on too long. 'I don't,' you say. 'I never seem to know.'

And I long to say that you will learn, but how can I, when I know nothing of it either.

This explains why the only reason we end is because you leave the city, the country.

All this while, you've been applying for a degree abroad, to a handful of universities. Gathering documents and recommendations, writing out statements of purpose, and sending them all off by special courier. Months later, the letters of acceptance (and one rejection) start coming in. You make your choice. This one, you declare. Now, you are heading home for a while, and then leaving for the city with a river. My year with you has come to a close. We don't talk about it, strangely enough, maybe because we always knew this had to end.

The night before you leave we order in and eat dinner around the heater that no longer needs to be switched on. We retreat to the couch, like we had on our first night together. The only glow comes from an outside street light, but it's enough for me to see the curve of your shoulders and breasts, the line of your neck when you lift your head in pleasure, the swell of your thighs. You still kiss me immensely, as though all your life you wouldn't kiss anyone else in the world. And for those moments, I feel loved. I hope you do too.

When I return to the flat a few days later, it is empty. The rooms displaying no evidence of your presence; your clothes gone, the shampoo sachets empty. I hadn't expected to find you there. I replace the sheets over the furniture. I move among them like a ghost.

THE UNDERTAKER

I FIRST NOTICE your knees, my love.

We meet in the kitchen the day after we've all moved in. The kitchen six of us share, students from different corners of the world. I have a crush on them all. Well, all the women. The man, Norwegian I think he said, I don't like so much. He has that cocky, white-boy air about him that I'm certain I will grow to detest. He is also very cheerful, which is annoying. The room opposite mine is occupied by a Cambodian–American. She is lovely, with a face like a soft full moon, thick eyebrows, full beautiful lips. She's quite young, and an exchange student, which means she will be here only a few months. The next set of rooms are occupied by the Norwegian, and a German with the blondest hair I've seen, and the bluest eyes. She's a walking Aryan cliché, but very pleasant. She has a boyfriend, I think. He leaves her room every morning. Closest to the main entrance door is

a Japanese student with hair straight and long like a dark waterfall, and, opposite her, you. You're beautiful otherwise as well, but like I said, I first notice your knees.

I'm cooking dinner, peppers stuffed with rice and meat, and you walk in, wine glass in hand. It's empty and you refill it from a bottle in the cupboard. Generously. To the top, like you're pouring out juice. I like you already.

You're wearing a shirt, a long, buttoned shirt that falls mid-thigh. You're not skinny, but your legs are slender, and your knees taut and well-shaped.

'Hi,' you say, and your first question is, 'Would you like some?' You hold out the wine bottle.

'Why not?'

We sit at the dining table, if it can be called that. An ugly metal-and-processed-wood contraption that has probably seen many student parties and not much cleaning. But it's placed by the window, and this city with a river offers us a view of a clock tower in the distance, and sharp roofs, and glimmering lights.

You tell me your name, I tell you mine.

You say you've never heard it before, that it is beautiful. I tell you my mother named me, and that it means nostalgia, because back home that is what we are all born into.

When we clink our glasses, we look into each other's eyes. I wonder if you have kissed a girl before.

'What do you study?' I ask.

'Comparative literature. And you?'

I tell you I'm an archivist of communities now. I used to be a lawyer, but I retired from that not so long ago.

For the first few weeks, we meet like this, casually in the kitchen, but each time we stay longer and longer to talk. I tell you funny stories about this bartender with dreadlocks I went out with on a date. You laugh and listen intently, but don't offer any stories in return.

'Do you have a boyfriend?' I ask finally. 'Girlfriend?' I casually add. You're sitting on the cooking counter, legs dangling. I'm roasting lamb in the oven.

'Neither.'

'But you wouldn't mind either?' I tease, poking the meat with a skewer. It's not done yet, I can tell even without doing this, but it gives me an excuse to bend over and not see your face.

'Not at all.' But the tone of your voice is light and airy. You could be joking.

One evening, you knock at my door. I open it, delighted. You stand there, unsure whether to enter. Our rooms are so tiny that more than one person inside inevitably feels like an intrusion. You're wondering whether I could help you top up your laundry card on my laptop. It's not happening on yours.

'Here.' You give me a ten-pound note.

'Habibi,' I say, 'first, come in. One never settles money matters like this...'

My room is neat, perhaps a little sparse. Your eyes flit across quickly and then settle on me. We sort out the top-up and, saying you must attend to your laundry, you leave.

Another night, emboldened, I knock on your door.

Unlike me, you have truly made the room your own. The large soft-board (mine's empty) is pinned with postcards and posters. A string of flower lights outlines the frame. From the smoke detector hang streamers with words. There's a painting of a tiger in the corner, red and black. And by your bedside you've placed a lamp. It's the only light that's on, and it imparts a soft, gentle glow. I am enamoured. It's like entering a world impossibly beautiful, and you have created it all with your own hands.

You're in bed, curled up, reading *Bonjour Tristesse*, when I enter.

'*Mon petit cheri...* for you there is only joy.'

'You must read this,' you say, sitting up. 'I'll give it to you when I'm done.' You ask me to sit. I'm uncertain whether I should perch at the edge of the bed, or the chair.

I draw up the chair.

'For you too there is only joy...' You say my name softly. Tenderly, I like to imagine. Suddenly, I almost cry.

You are quick to notice. 'Are you all right?'

I nod, and smile.

After this, I come to your room often. Sometimes, we sit in silence, reading, working on assignments. Sometimes, we talk. We share things I'd like to think we haven't shared with anyone before. You ask if I'm close to my parents. I am. And you? You are not. At first, I think you don't speak of this with much difficulty, but I notice that when you tell me about them, it sounds almost rehearsed. Like a speech you've prepared in your head. 'I've grown up away from them... they were part-time parents if there's such a thing... it doesn't matter, of course. I love them and all that... but I guess I don't know them. And they don't know me at all.' I want to ask if this bothers you, but beyond this you seem to clam up. At other times, we talk about past loves. We discover we've both been with someone who was married. With someone whom we just couldn't bring ourselves to leave despite all common sense.

Neither of us have had one-night stands. Yet.

So we make an amorous pact. Before our year here is up, we tell each other, laughing. I almost did once, I tell you. I went home with this South African man, to his place far to the south of the river, but I backed out and left his flat in the middle of the night. He wasn't pleased, and he never called me again.

'Why did you change your mind?' you ask.

Truthfully, I say I don't know.

I tell you about everyone except my last love. It is too soon to speak of him.

Often, we venture to a coffee shop, and work in a corner. We look nice together, I think. Our dark heads bent over notes and books. I wear glasses. You don't. We dress similarly, in jeans, boots, heavy, chunky sweaters, and quilted jackets against the cold. I notice you like hats. I smoke. You don't, but occasionally you sneak a puff. You like cats. I don't. Once, when we are on our way to the café, you're unusually quiet. I ask if everything's okay. I expect you to say you're struggling with deadlines, or are having trouble with an assignment, but it has nothing to do with university.

'It's very silly...' you begin. Which is when I know it isn't.

'I got an email... from this guy... one of many, actually...'

'Many guys?'

You laugh. 'No, emails.'

I say there is only one reason why people write emails any more. Apart from work, that is.

'Which is?'

'To break up with someone.'

'Or to try and make up?'

'Which one is it?'

The latter, you say. 'It's so weird... because he's the one who broke up with me... I told you, remember? And now suddenly this...'

'He came right out and said it?'

'Pretty much.'

'Is this the guy you couldn't bring yourself to leave?'

You nod. I study your face, but you can sometimes be impassive.

We are at the coffee shop, and order our usual: a large flat black for me, milky cappuccino for you, and a cherry almond muffin to share. As we make our way downstairs to our usual spot, I ask, 'What is he like?'

'Impassioned.'

'Do you still like him?'

You take a moment to reply. 'I haven't thought about him in a long time... I don't know why he would do this...'

'What exactly did his email say?'

'That he misses me... and is wondering what I'm doing... and that he thinks he made a mistake... and would I like to meet up, even if just for old times' sake...'

I sip my coffee. It isn't as strong as I like it but it'll do. 'And what will you do?'

You suddenly look stricken. 'I don't know... for now, I think, nothing...'

'The most important question, though, is...'

'What?' You look utterly, immovably serious.

'Was the sex good?'

After this, we cannot stop laughing.

One evening, I knock at your door because I want to tell you about my dead lover, but you're not in. And the next time, when I'm in your room because you've invited me to watch a funny video, it doesn't seem quite appropriate. How to say,

'He died, you know,' as we giggle over a panda behaving badly in a zoo.

So it happens that I tell you in the kitchen. When something the white boy said has upset me. A sexist, racist comment that makes me want to smash his face through the window. Instead, I wash my dishes violently, the water spilling over the edges of the sink, splashing to the floor. A glass slips from my grip, hits the edge, and breaks.

'Fuck...' I swear.

'What happened?' You appear behind me.

'I will kill him, that... that little...'

'Shit?' you offer helpfully. 'What did he say?'

That he's always wanted to ask an Arab woman out on a date but he's worried he's not wealthy enough.

You stay silent, but I can see anger in your eyes. Your fingers clench the edge of the table, knuckles white. Then finally, in a voice that's unnaturally light-hearted, you say, 'Shall we go to the pub and discuss ways to wreak vengeance? Or shall we just go to the pub anyway, because he's not worth our time or energy.' You move closer. 'He's not worth our anger even.'

I can see what you're trying to do, to deflect and distract, because sometimes the encounter with something so twisted and deep-seated deserves not much more than a scornful laugh. But tonight, I cannot. I am upset, I have been crying in my room. It has been three months, and the day that

marked the anniversary went uncommemorated. It passed like all other days do, and, I've realised, so will all others. I cannot bear it, I just cannot.

'I wouldn't be like this if... if...' And I almost cry. 'He hadn't died.'

You don't comprehend, of course. Who died, who he is, was, or what he means, to me.

I tell you he was a photographer, and that I met him at the house of a writer friend back home. He was tall, with a beautiful smile. I would sneak out to see him during lunch hour at the NGO I worked in, in the old city. We were very different – he was outgoing and had a thousand friends, while I could count my closest on one hand – but somehow it worked. He liked my quietness, he told me, and I loved his joy, his ability to meet each day with the same amount of untiring enthusiasm as the last. It seemed boundless. But there were times when we were out of sync, his energy and mine. The last time I saw him, we fought.

'Why?'

Over some silly thing about going out to meet friends, at some party or the other. I walked out of his house, even though he came to the front door, calling for me, saying it was okay, we could stay home. And usually I would relent and turn back, but that evening I kept going all the way home. It was probably a Sunday, and I would have been busy at work the next day. He didn't call. I didn't call.

What I do remember is receiving the news, and disbelieving it all. It was his heart, they said.

His heart? It was large and strong and infinite. I had lain my head on his chest and listened to it many times. The thud of it against my ear, its double percussion. I stayed disbelieving until I saw him lying in a box.

The only sound in the kitchen is the dripping of the tap behind me. I've abandoned the dishes, the broken glass. My hands are covered in soapsuds, and slippery.

'He was older than me, but too young to be dead.'

'I'm sorry,' I hear you murmur. 'I'm sorry.'

The lights in the kitchen are white and harsh, like in a hospital. I ask if we can talk elsewhere; we go to your room. We walk silently, a funeral procession. We sit on your bed. Despite the cold, the window is open and there's a river breeze.

'You know what is the strangest thing?'

You watch me without saying a word.

'That I could remember the feel of his skin, the warmth... I couldn't stop thinking about the time we'd spent together... not on the streets, or in restaurants and clubs, but in bed. Because I suppose that was the most physical, most alive thing... and it was gone. Have you ever had a lover who's died?'

You shake your head. 'It must be hardest to lose someone that way.'

'That's what you would think, no? That this person is forever... gone. Out of your life in the most permanent way possible. But I feel... or at least I've come to believe that it's harder knowing that the person you are no longer with is somewhere laughing, eating, sleeping... doing all these mundane things, and carrying on with life. Maybe for me that's also consolation. The shock of losing... of course that is harder when they die. But you know, selfishly, they will never be anyone else's but yours.' I try and smile, but it must come out looking horrible, because you turn away, and take my hand instead.

At first, I don't tell you everything.

That for months after his death, I used to wake up at night shaking.

That back at home, before I moved here, I walked past his house every evening, even though it wasn't on my way back from work. That I used to go to his grave, and place my palm on the ground just as I used to on his chest.

I am grateful for being away, for being caught up in a new place, in studying, but there are things you carry with you always. The night, for me, will never be the same again. It has become a length of time within which you can lose the unimaginable. I still wake up shivering, and I dream often that I am watching him leave, on a bus, a train, that I am being abandoned.

But you have a way of drawing things out of me by not asking too much, for that would be like approaching a bird in haste and frightening it away. Instead I find things left outside my door – a chocolate in the shape of an egg, a clipping about the world's oldest tree, a postcard of some place by the sea, a white origami bird. I am secretly pleased to see you don't take the trouble to do this for any of the others.

Slowly, I get to know you better too.

I know you are kind, my love, but prone to spells of strange quietude. When no one, no matter how close, is welcome. Once, I found out for myself, when I knocked at your door, and you opened it as though to a stranger.

'Yes?'

I didn't know how to reply, or what to ask. 'It's me,' I felt like saying. Not that you didn't speak to me, but you did so so grudgingly that I slunk away.

You are brave.

There are many things I will remember about you, but this in particular.

We were taking a walk one afternoon, and a rugged dog on the pavement, whose owner could barely control him, barked and strained at me on the leash. He came close to snapping at my leg, but you stepped between us, waving your bag at the beast.

'Shooooooh...' you yelled, 'Shoooohhhh...'

And rather than being frightened, I watched you, the look on your face, intent, furious, waving a magic circle of protection around us. The dog barked at you, but you didn't flinch. Then he retreated, the owner dragging him away, apologising profusely.

'Thank you,' I said.

'For what?' You flicked your hair aside, and continued walking.

You are tall, but I am slightly taller, and you are more slender than me.

I suppose some may consider it a small thing, but for that moment, when you stood between me and the dog, I felt as though nothing could harm or touch me, not even death.

I am in love with you by way of deepest, most profound friendship.

Does that make sense? It does to me.

We sit for long hours late into the night in your room, talking. I tell you stories about my home, how it has been taken away, mutilated. I come, I tell you, from one of the most troubled parts of the world, where it is easier to live in hate and suspicion than to love. It is hard to love under subjugation. Every little bit of tenderness is a miracle. And my photographer, with his easy laughter, helped remind me of what could be normal. 'Now he too is gone.' It is impossible for anything tender to survive. You listen with

your heart. You are good at that too. Generous, giving. Sometimes reaching out to touch my hand, my shoulder. Never before, you say, have you thought about how much you take for granted. Once, you place your palm on my cheek. We are close enough to kiss. But you lie back, leaning against your pillow, closing your eyes.

'You are beautiful.'

You look at me. 'And you. And you.'

One day we decide to head to the north of the city, to a heath, we've heard, that stretches for miles and miles. We take the underground. As we slide down on the escalator, we watch the advertising squares glide past us. A new musical in the West End, an exhibition on the royal family, life insurance, lingerie.

'She's gorgeous,' I say of the woman in the picture. She's wearing a lacy purple bra and panties. Curvy and soft, ripe with fullness.

You agree.

'Would you like to fuck her?' I ask.

You lean closer. 'Many, many times.'

Others would say you're a tease, but I like you too much. Often, I think it's preferable, this constant anticipation. Being perpetually on a pleasurable edge.

Perhaps it's the only way to retain it. Love. To never have it happen. To love, otherwise, is always to lose. And

isn't it true? That one imagined kiss is worth a thousand real ones.

I say this also to console myself.

At the heath, in an open field, we find a giant chair and table.

It is wooden, and it looms over us, tall as a building.

People are playing football between the legs, and picnicking in its shade.

'It is an artwork,' you tell me.

'Signifying what?'

'Whatever you wish it to.' Nowadays, you add, everything is non-essentialist.

We circle it innumerable times, and each time it changes. First, it symbolises all of literature. Everything ever written, collected, towering above us into the sky. Then it's the work desk of a giant. A badly designed alien spaceship. Jesus' DIY Father's Day gift. We laugh until people around us stare. For a second, I want to hold your face between my hands and smash my mouth to yours. Your fingers graze mine, intertwine, and you don't release them.

'Who will make me laugh,' you ask, 'when you leave?'

Our year-long programmes end in three months. I will head home. The piece of paper in my passport demands it.

'Will you too?'

You nod. But first you will be in the countryside for a while, with some friends you know from home. But I'm not interested in that. I care only for the time we have together.

'We have a summer.'

'You have a summer to make me laugh.'

And a summer can be a lifetime.

We walk a path that takes us into the woods. It is darker here, and colder. The air changes. It's heavier and wet, like something ancient. The trees are still, as in a painting. The leaves beneath our feet squelch and slide in the mud. Soon, we come to a clearing which is all our own. We sit on a bench, dedicated to the heath in memory of someone named Diana, 'who so loved it here'. We can see the sky. It is darkening yet clear, still tinged with the long-lost blue of the day.

'Did you ever reply to that email?' I ask.

You nod.

'What did you write?'

'Well... I told him first of all that I was away...'

'And will you meet him when you're back?'

'Maybe...'

I tell you about an internet meme I saw that said getting back together with an ex is like reusing old underwear after a shower. We laugh. Then we sit in silence as twilight settles around us.

'Look,' you say, pointing to the sky.

In the distance, there's a group of birds, about a hundred or more. They drop and rise, changing formation in waves like water. Following an invisible, secret pattern known only to them and their wings. We watch them circle and swoop, toss and tail. It is endlessly fascinating.

'What are they?' I ask. I have never seen such a thing, such creatures.

They are starlings, you say, and you are certain they are the souls of the dead.

My voice is stuck in my throat. I'd like to think that's true.

That all the dead in the world are reborn into creatures of flight.

THE PROFESSOR

WE ARE TALKING about tuna at the table.

I think it's ridiculous there's such a thing as sustainable fishing. That's why we have farms, I explain. Tuna farms, or fisheries or whatever they're called. Sustainable fishing is a label they slap on so that they can charge five times the price.

You are livid.

'That's not the point,' you say.

Then what is? I ask. I'm rather enjoying how annoyed you look.

I'm told there is a larger picture I'm ignoring.

I think there's a silent insinuation that I'm stupid. (I'm hurt. I'm the youngest here, but I know I'm not stupid.)

To fish sustainably would mean less dependence on, or requirement of, fish farms, you continue. Why that's important I fail to see, but I allow you to carry on. I like the sound of your voice, especially when it's tinged with anger.

You sound clipped, and crisp, and your tone deepens. You don't say much otherwise; this is the only time I've heard you speak at some length. Ever since we were introduced a few days ago, I've done most of the talking.

I've told you how I always spend my mid-term break at this house, owned by these friends of yours, because my mother is far away in the unfashionable east of the continent. Also, it's not much fun going home. That part of the world is dull and grey, and I'm not only talking about the weather. I like staying here. Your friends are kind to me; they give me the attic, and I can do what I like. I can turn up the radio. Or read aloud while I'm studying. Although I think that bothers you. You are in the room right below mine, and you don't sit there and read any more, I've noticed.

You told me you were finishing your postgraduate degree. I told you I was finishing school ('Really?' You thought I was older, which pleased me) and had just applied to one of the oldest universities in the world.

'To study what?' you asked.

'Physics.'

I don't know why, but you didn't ask me any more questions after that.

Let me tell you that I've never had time for girls before. I attend an all-boys school, I work hard, I hate sports and television. My father left when I was eight, my mother

suffers from paranoia (she calls every day at 8 a.m. and 8 p.m.). Very little has made sense to me except physics, the basic principles that govern the physical world around us. Momentum, forces, motion, energy. Everything can be explained. Eventually.

Even this, what I feel for you.

At first, nothing. You walk in with your bag in the middle of the afternoon. I'm listening to the radio in the living room and barely notice you. This house is what my hosts like to call an 'open house', so there is always someone coming or going or passing through for a meal. I'm used to it. I notice only your eyes. Then you're swept off by our hosts, to your room below mine, and then you're in the kitchen, chatting, offering to help out with the evening meal. I go back upstairs to study. At dinner, we are opposite each other at the table. I'm allowed a small glass of wine. You, I notice, drink quickly, one and then another. You will be drunk and disorderly soon, I think silently, but you are impeccably composed. I am asked what I've been doing all day, and I tell them, but I don't think you're interested. You concentrate on the food on your plate, on refilling glasses with wine. This is annoying. I decide not to be interested in you either.

Over the next couple of days, we're usually the only ones at home. Our hosts leave for work early. You're meant to be

working on your dissertation – I think you said you were studying literature (another one of those things that make little sense to me) – but that's mostly a laugh. I hear you at the piano (your playing is barely competent, I'm afraid), or see you sleeping on the couch, or browsing the bookshelf lining the corridor. It's wide and large, almost from floor to ceiling and you work your way across it slowly. I recognise none of the books you pull out, except perhaps the Iliad, and only because I was forced to study it in school. The problem with literature, I tell you over lunch (ham sandwiches and soup), is that it's always so out of time.

You stare at me like I'm the village idiot before you ask, 'Why?'

'Because no matter how much we make of universality, a book is always written in a particular place and time. It cannot be read as it's being written. Ever after, the text is out of date. Literature is always past.'

'Literature,' you say coldly, 'is not the news.'

'But you miss what I mean,' I say. 'We think that books can offer us insights into human behaviour, but is that really true? When every situation, every person, is undeniably individual.'

'That is not literature's claim,' you say, your voice betraying the smallest tremor of anger. 'There are...'

'Patterns?' I complete.

'Yes, patterns.'

'Even these "patterns" we speak of, that the great classics are said to offer, are just that. A sort of hope of making sense of arbitrary actions, of unpredictable reasoning, of incredible randomness. All literature, apart from offering partially competent documentation, is useless.'

(I'm enjoying this, even if you are not.)

I wait for you to react, to fling your sandwich at me, to drench my head with carrot soup, but you eat quietly, methodically, and when you finish, say, 'Suit yourself.' I take it you are not the argumentative type. I admit I'm disappointed. Except the next day you argue eloquently, fiercely, about sustainable fishing. Perhaps the freedom of tuna to swim the open seas is dearer to you than the Iliad. You delight and confuse me.

But I don't feel in this strange way for you until I see you almost naked. It's true. It is late, and I'm in my room, studying, and I need to use the loo, which is annoying because I must go downstairs. The bathroom is next to your room; we must share, and all these few days it's been fine, because somehow we've never needed to use it at the same time. Except tonight. I'm halfway down the stairs when the bathroom door opens and you step out. You've just had a shower; your hair is wet, but swept up untidily, loosening around the edges. Your shoulders are bare and glistening. You've wrapped a towel around you loosely. It reaches your knees. I see you from above, and suddenly cannot breathe.

I have never felt this way before. It's not as though I haven't seen skimpily clad women – at least in pictures (I study in an all-boys school, remember?) – but I'd see them and think, what's all the fuss about?

You, though, are as beautiful as light splitting through glass.

I don't know how you know I'm there; I'd stepped down noiselessly, but you look up and see me, and for a moment we're both transfixed. You lift a hand to your heart and smile, and I smile back.

After this, like some stupid helpless puppy, I constantly need to know where you are. As though I am oriented only by your presence, or your absence. You are my north.

It is undoubtedly odd. I find it difficult also to keep silent; I talk and talk because I want you to feel like it would be rude to leave the room.

I want you to take me everywhere.

One afternoon, I meet you on your way out. 'For a walk,' you say when I enquire where you're going. I ask if I may come along, and I'm thrilled when you acquiesce. I think you like my company after all, else you would have said no.

'Where are we going?' We've walked along the main road and then turned off on to a country path.

'I have no idea.'

This makes me nervous. I begin to say there are maps back in the house; we can plot a route, pick up a book on local walks. You laugh, and that settles it.

The day is nice, I suppose. I'm not good at describing things. They are just as they are. But it feels like summer. With the sunshine and the shade, and everything rich and green. I've seen a few winters here, and this is its very opposite. You delight in everything. Some flowers growing on the roadside, the hedge with blossoms that smell of honey, some flitting butterfly.

'Is this your first summer here?' I ask tentatively.

You nod.

I want to tell you all about it, but something nudges me to keep quiet, and I do.

Instead, I ask how you know our hosts.

You say you often volunteered at a charity school they were running back in your home country. For an unfathomable reason, you add, 'They're like my parents.'

We walk along, rarely passed by cars or other pedestrians. It's the middle of the week. We could be the only ones in the whole world. I have not felt this way before. No, actually I have. I spent one holiday alone in school because my hosts were not in the country, and I did not wish to go back home. I woke up to silence, and empty classrooms and corridors and playing fields. It was a day gift-wrapped for me, a present waiting under a tree, and the same with this one, for us, you and me.

The path we are on rises and dips, every slope eliciting pleasure from you – a particular view of hills, a sprawling

oak, an old farmhouse. Then we pass an open field with a horse grazing. She's a muted gold with a white mane and tail, and stands before a high hedge, in silvery grass. You call it a scene out of a painting.

'Oh,' you say, leaning on the fence, 'what shall we name her?'

I struggle to think of something. I'm not in the habit of naming horses, or anything else for that matter, but I try.

'Scăpăra.'

You turn to me, puzzled, surprised. 'What's that?'

'In my language it means to strike fire.'

'Scăpăra,' you repeat, and I help you pronounce the word correctly. 'Scăpăra... lovely.' And you smile.

Our walk ends at a pub.

It's late afternoon by then, and you announce, after checking your phone and sending several messages back and forth, that our hosts will pick us up from there on their way home from work. I'm relieved; I didn't wish to walk back all the way. Already I'd mentioned a few times that my feet were aching, that we should have brought along some water because it was warm and we could get dehydrated. You seemed not the least bit concerned.

At the bar, I order a cranberry juice, and you a pint of local cider. We settle at a table by the window. Outside is an empty car park ringed by trees. At our feet lie Layla and

Gramsci, the resident dogs, a black Labrador and a golden retriever. You pet them fearlessly. I try to make myself smaller in the corner.

'Come,' you say, 'they're gentle creatures.'

I admit I'm petrified of all animals.

'Did you not have pets while growing up?'

A goldfish once, which I found one morning floating belly up. I was seven; it was the scariest thing I'd seen. But horses, I say belatedly, I like.

On some evenings, you and our hosts hold long conversations at the dining table, or in the living room. After dinner, when I've usually trooped back up to my attic to study. But I'm curious. What could you all be talking about? When I stay back, hovering in the kitchen, or the corridor lined with books, I discover it's you. There's some on-going crisis. At least that's what it sounds like.

'They just don't understand... neither do they listen...' you say mutinously.

'The important thing,' our hosts advise, 'is you do what you feel is right for you now, at this point...'

'I can't believe they want me to find a job... any job...'

'Not any job, surely...'

'It's true... anything will do... even some data-entry rubbish... anything that'll keep me in this country... because they've spent all this money for me to study here... and it would be a waste to leave and go back...'

'But why would it be a waste?'

'I don't know...' You sound exasperated. I imagine you pacing the room in anger.

'And if you go back...?'

'They'll be livid...' And you laugh. 'Can you imagine? Even now, they treat me like this... expecting constant deference to their requests.'

At some point, say our hosts, we all anger our parents. There's no escaping it. Either you'll do it now, or later. But happen it will.

I sense you calm down. 'That's true,' you say.

There's a clink of bottle against glass, wine refilled, and the conversation meanders elsewhere.

Mostly, I'm a restless sleeper, but one night it's worse because earlier that evening I found a beast in my room. It flapped right past me when I entered; I hadn't even turned the light on. I screamed. I thought it was a ghost for certain, but no, we find a small, furry creature with wings. Somehow a bat had flown into the house. How bizarre, our hosts exclaimed, it's never happened before.

That night, I cannot sleep.

Until I came to study here a few years ago, I'd been scared of the dark. And the fears return. I hear wings and strange flutters. I don't know how late it is when I walk down the stairs, thinking I'll get a glass of water. The door to your room

is ajar. I don't pass it on my way, but I walk towards it. How do you sleep? I imagine you on your back, your head turned on the pillow, the blanket up to your chest, the rise and fall of your breath. Instead, you are sitting up in bed. Breathing deeply as though you just woke up from a nightmare. You look up and don't seem surprised to see me standing there.

'I thought I heard a noise.'

'I'm sorry... did I wake you?'

'No... not at all... I was going downstairs... to the kitchen...'

You don't seem to be listening.

I walk closer, tentatively; I stop at the foot of the bed. 'Are you all right?'

'It was horrible,' you whisper.

'Did you have a bad dream?'

You nod.

'What did you see?'

'I was running...'

I don't tell you that that doesn't sound particularly scary.

'I don't know what was following me... but I just knew somehow I was in danger... and that I needed to reach some house in the distance... and when I got there...'

You look at me stricken.

'When you got there?'

'I knocked on the door... and someone opened it and said I could come in... but only if I was an orphan...'

I don't say it was just a dream. Because my mother would say that to me, and it never helped.

A dream, I know all too well, is real.

I sit tentatively at the edge of the bed; I'm close enough to see beads of sweat on your forehead, even though the nights here are always chilly. Any other time I can talk, but it's at moments like these that I don't know what to say, or how to offer comfort. So I sit there in stupid silence. I would like to reach out and take your hand, or touch your shoulder. Instead, I reach out to the carafe on the nightstand and pour you a glass of water. You sip gingerly.

'Thank you.' You look up and for a moment, in that stillness, in that darkness and our proximity, I think you might kiss me. What a foolish, foolish wish.

Then, as I am about to stand and make my way out, you reach for my arm. Your touch is warm, warmer than a leaf in the sun.

'Do you think... you could stay... a while?'

I nod.

'I used to have many bad dreams too...' I don't know why I'm telling you this. 'Especially after my dad left.' I think it's because I want you to know I understand, and I have nothing else to offer.

You look at me a long while, and then lift your hand to my cheek. I sit perfectly still, like I've turned to stone. I'm a bat in the corner, fearful of being found.

'You couldn't fall asleep tonight?'

'No.'

You don't ask why. Instead, you shift to make room in your bed. There's space for me only because you lie on your side. I lie down next to you, your breath close on my neck; you smell of moss and grapefruit and early summer.

I don't dare move, in case we touch, in case you feel me. My body, this thing I hardly think about, what I've mostly considered a vessel for my mind, betrays me. I close my eyes, as though if I don't see, you won't either, but that's worse, because now I see you in a towel, lifting your hand to your heart, and dropping it loose. I have never known my mind to disobey me as much as when I tell it to think of something else.

Suddenly you ask, 'Is this strange?'

And in my nervousness, I begin to tell you that in physics 'strangeness' is actually a property of particles. That strange quarks are unstable subatomic particles that decay into an up quark, an electron, and an electron antineutrino. That they have long lifetimes... and are usually formed in pairs. At this, I look at you because I think you are choking. No, you're laughing. Your head thrown back on your pillow. You drape an arm across my face, draw me closer, and kiss the top of my head. You nuzzle into my shoulder, closing your eyes.

'We're a pair of strange quarks.'

I have never been happier. I have never been sadder.

JANICE PARIAT

On your last day with us, our hosts think it a splendid idea to take us for a picnic to the coast. I go only because of you. I dislike picnics and sand and sun.

'Will you come along?' our hosts ask in surprise.

'Yes,' I say. 'I think it might be a nice change.'

'We think so too,' they say, thrilled, because they, like most people on this island, are fond of what they call 'the great outdoors'. They hike and camp and go swimming. (I've been told I'm as pale as garlic, but I don't, as they say here, give a shit.)

After a delayed start – the basket couldn't be found, the mayonnaise was dropped and had to be remade from scratch, the scones wouldn't rise – we finally head out. The coast is an hour's drive away through the countryside, and even I have to admit it looks picturesque. You and our hosts talk about the books that have been written by a famous writer in the area; I have nothing to add, so I look out of the window and stay quiet. Also, I'm trying not to think about how, from tomorrow, you will be gone. When we finally turn off the main road and come to the end of the rough path to the coast, we are all pinned – yes, that's the word I would use, as though we're butterflies caught by a lepidopterist – by the astonishing view of water. Well, you all are.

I sneak glances at you. We tumble out of the car, hamper and all, and walk to the beach, which, I assure you, is far from tropical. Instead, there's curiously smooth shingle beneath our feet.

'Storm-weathered,' you say. 'It's against the law to pick them up and take them away.'

There, we meet our hosts' friends, who've already picked a spot, and laid out a blanket, and food and drinks.

I think I will faint from the heat. Except everyone else looks so thrilled by the weather that it might be pointless to complain. You are in a dress with straps tied behind your neck, and a large straw hat. I don't like wearing shorts so I've rolled up my trousers to my knees, and my tee shirt, I'm sure, will soon be soaked in unsightly sweat. I notice that you too are slightly cautious of venturing too close to the water, and my heart soars. We stand at the edge, just beyond the reach of the waves; to our sides the coastline opens like endless wings. (I find it hard to believe I said that. But sometimes I like to think I can look at the world the way I suspect you do. If I could be poetic, sometimes, perhaps you'd take more notice of me.) We don't see it coming, and when we do it's too late. The wave, suddenly higher and stronger than all the others, almost knocks us off our feet. It's so quick that we exclaim, startled, and then laugh, because no harm has been done.

'Look.' You are holding out your hand.

On your palm, a starfish.

'It's been tossed out of the ocean... and found its way to me.'

We examine it closely; you are amazed at its intricacy and beaded skin. I am more taken by the smell of lemons rising from your hair.

'What shall we do with it?' you ask. 'I feel as though I've been given a... gift.'

We look at each other, and then at the tiny creature, and we both know. You bend, and wait until the water laps over your hands and feet. When the wave recedes, your palm is empty.

We are called back to the others for food and drink. I cannot understand this love for boiled eggs and pickled onions. I help myself to ham and bread instead. You pick at the fruit and cheese. You are quiet, I notice, and I long to somehow cheer you up. You drain one beer, and then another; I'm allowed a glass of white wine. Someone brings out a board game. I blanch. So, I'm relieved to see, do you.

You excuse yourself, saying something about taking a walk, and I scramble up to join you. The pebbles crunch beneath our feet. We walk a mile or so in silence, passing a fisherman, and then another. Then it's just the beach and sky and water and us.

You stop. 'Do you know what I'd like to do?'

Kiss me.

You pick a stone, smooth and curved, and walk to the water's edge. I have no idea what you're attempting, until you

bend and fling your arm back and then forward. The stone skips once and sinks. You laugh, I laugh, and I suddenly remember my father doing the same, at a river back in my country, when I was very young and he hadn't yet left us.

'You try,' you shout.

And I hesitate. My father hadn't stayed long enough to teach me.

But you are suddenly boisterous and happy, and I cannot let you down. You help me pick a stone and show me how to squat low. You're a terrible teacher. Our stones sink one after another. Our greatest achievement is two skips, maybe three.

This, you declare, must be the oldest game in the world.

Along with, I say, hide-and-seek.

For those moments, we are children. I feel I haven't been a child in a long time.

Then I remember that soon you will be gone, and I feel like a child about to be abandoned.

When we finish, after exhausting all the suitably shaped stones around us, we stand and watch the water, calm now like glass. The sky is gathering clouds and has darkened, and when you leave it will rain.

THE BUTCHER

You get in touch long after you return from the city with a river.

Like a year or something. It's a lazy Sunday afternoon, I'm home, you call, and we end up saying things over the phone that make me shut my bedroom door and drop my pyjamas.

How did it happen?

I don't know. I think it began when I asked what you were doing, and you said you were in bed, under a sheet, naked.

It's been ages since we met or spoke, but the sex is, as always, good.

Funnily enough, it's awkward when we meet.

We sit across the table, holding our coffees, which you said you'd prefer to evening drinks, and we find, at first, little to say. You've cut your hair short. It's drastic but looks great. I tell you so. You smile and say I'm looking good too.

'So, how are...'

'How have you...'

We speak at the same time. We laugh.

You first, you say graciously.

And I tell you that I've finished with film school, and set up my own small production house. That I freelance mostly, moving from project to project. Then I look up at you shyly and say, 'But the best news is that I went ahead and started a band.'

'Oh, that's fantastic,' you say, and I think you sound genuinely happy for me. Except maybe the look in your eyes doesn't quite match your smile.

'And you?'

You tell me you're managing all right now, but it hasn't been easy. 'With work,' you add as though you're worried I might think otherwise. When you returned after completing your studies, you had to find a job in some hurry.

'Why was that?' I asked.

You say something airily about your parents, that they weren't too pleased.

'That their daughter returned from "foreign"?' I can't help grinning. I've met your parents briefly. I didn't like them, they didn't like me. I know they have their sights and ambitions set on places far and away.

You nod. 'They told me they found this decision difficult to support.' Then you roll your eyes. It's such a familiar

gesture. I can hear you say it in your head: *As though they know anything about me.*

'So did you find a job quickly?'

You did, but the small design house you joined as a content writer, run by a shady businessman, didn't pay you for months. So you quit and worked with a city magazine, tramping through the streets in the heat, doing stories on the best cutlets and where to get a bespoke suit stitched.

'That sounds fun...'

'It was, for a while... then they shut down.'

'What?'

You look up and laugh. 'Apparently everything's going online.'

'Then what did you do?'

You say you joined an academic publishing house, and almost died of boredom. That you now know more about import–export laws than you ever cared to. We're chatting like old friends, which I suppose, in a way, we are. At the moment, you tell me, you're attached to a book house, run by one of these foreign cultural institutes in the city. It pays well, the hours are light, and you get to attend events with freely flowing wine. For a while, we are still and silent, and the city hums around us. I wonder if you'll ask me about the emails I'd sent you while you were away. I hope you don't because I wouldn't know what to say now, with us here, face-to-face.

'You're lucky, you know,' you say suddenly.

'Why?'

'Because you've always known what you want to do.'

This is odd, and touching, and I want to lean in and stroke your hand, or arm, or cheek.

'And you... don't?'

'Not really, no. I'm quite...' But you don't complete your sentence.

'You're quite...?'

You shake your head, and smile, and the word is lost.

It's easier for us to hook up, because you're living on your own now.

I'm still with flatmates in another part of town, and believe me, it's not a pretty sight. You live in a tiny but comfortable barsati, one of those top-floor flats with two rooms and a large terrace. There's a bright yellow sofa, a large shelf of books, an old-fashioned work desk, on the wall a black-and-red painting of a tiger and photographs of your time in the city with a river. But you might never have been gone, because I'm surprised by how easily and quickly it happens. Although if our phone conversation was any indication, I suppose it couldn't be any other way. First though, we sit in your room and exchange stories. Who have we been with? It's like some sort of exorcism ritual. A naming of names. I've been with someone I worked with on a film, and it was only meant to last the length of the shoot, but it didn't. Then

from her side there was growing attachment. 'Where is this going?' she would ask afterwards, when we lay on the bed, side by side, and I would have no answer, and eventually she said she couldn't do this any more. I'd also been with some stranger I met on holiday at a beachside place. At least I think so. I'd drunk so much that day my memory fails me. Then there was a car ride I'd taken with some old college friends. They'd been drinking more than me, the girls on either side, and then they kissed and turned to me. But relationships? Nothing lasting or significant. When I look at you and say it's your turn, you are quiet for a long while.

'Someone... much older... who I was with for a year... no one else...'

I say you're not getting away that easily. You smile. Does it count, you ask, if it's a crush on a girl who was your flatmate?

I say it certainly does. And nothing more? What about one-night stands?

You flush, and I long to kiss you. All this talk has left me with a funny quiver in my stomach.

Once, you say, before you left the city with a river. You and your flatmate had gone out drinking, and there was this guy at the wine bar...

'You went home with?'

You nod.

'To his place?'

You nod again.

You'd never done anything like that before, you say, which you suppose was precisely what drove you to do it.

'It wasn't very wise, was it?' I can hear myself say. I can't help feel a little jealous, a little judgemental even.

You frown. 'What do you mean?'

'Well... going home with some stranger... who knows what could've happened?'

'He lived alone,' you offer.

'That's even worse.' I'm almost shouting now. I stand and pace the room. You watch me in silence.

'So,' I eventually ask, 'did it make you feel good? All young and reckless?'

'It was horrible actually,' you say quietly.

Something about the tone of your voice makes me stop and sit next to you. 'Why?'

You shrug. 'He had a girlfriend... there was a picture of her on his bedside table...'

'But nothing... happened to you, right?'

'No. Except...' you hesitate. 'Walking out of his house to the station the next morning, I wished it would rain...'

When we kiss after, it's hot and urgent, as though we need to make up for lost time. Your lips are strange and familiar all at once, like a song I've known well and somehow forgotten. We find our way around each other hesitantly, then easily, in sudden recognition. I remember what you like and you do too. There's a thrill though, of us not being the

same people, of our skins having changed, of our mouths being the same.

This second getting together is peaceful. Or at least it seems so.

I'm hopeful it will last. Perhaps we've grown wiser, more mature, and the rips and tears have healed. We go on quietly with our work, and do some old things and some new. Check out eating joints that have just opened, go for open-air concerts, visit a book market in the north of the city, go for long bike rides at night. You get a cat, or rather you find one abandoned in a dumpster near the market where you go shopping for groceries. She's the colour of smoke, and prettily striped in black, and tiny. She fits in the palm of your hand. You get her a hot-water bag, and a box, and line it with one of your old sweaters. From the pet store you buy her kitten feed and, on an impulse, a little red collar with a bell, and a toy mouse. You're thrilled to have her in your home. Soon, I too begin spending more time there, with the cat and you. I'm almost afraid to say it, but we're like a small family.

The cat is ridiculous.

We name her Muji.

When Muji's stronger, she gets up to all sorts of antics. You play with her for hours, and at night she curls up in the crook of your neck to keep warm. I don't know how you

feel about me, but you're definitely in love with Muji. And I am, admittedly, a little bit too. Unlike most cats, she has a trusting way about her, like a dog. Such naive affection. The kind that will get her into trouble someday. She rushes to greet us, or anyone else who comes to the house, happy to see everyone. She purrs, and arches her back, and digs her tiny paws into our chests and arms when we're in bed. She circles our ankles, and head-butts our shins. And sometimes when we address her, she chatters back in little mews. It's fucking adorable.

On occasion, I get to attend some of the cultural institute events you're invited to. It's all quite annoyingly posh, but the alcohol's free, so who's complaining? I don't give a shit about dress code, but you do. And this is where the cracks, fine as they are, reappear.

'You're going like that?'

I look down at my faded jeans and tie-dye tee-shirt. Perfectly acceptable evening attire, I think.

'Yes... I am...'

'Can't you wear a shirt...? And trousers? I know you hate to, but it's quite a formal evening...'

'Either they let me in like this... or I don't go...'

You roll your eyes. I hate it when you do that. 'It's not just about you... you're my guest, remember?'

I shrug. 'Then don't take me along.'

I don't understand why this is such a big deal for you. It's just a silly get-together over I don't even know what, and who cares what I wear?

From then on, the slide is gradual but unmistakable.

The next disagreement, bigger, brasher, more hurtful, happens when you tell me a film-maker friend is looking for someone to be cameraman on a shoot in the mountains. He's working for a well-established activist, and has many connections in the city, and it would be good for me to join their team. I share in your excitement. This could be a welcome break for me. So I get in touch with him via email, asking for details and rates. When he replies, I shut the laptop and tell you it isn't going to work out.

'Why?'

'Because he expects me to do this for free...'

'Oh, but that's okay... you'll gain experience and...'

'Exposure,' I finish for you.

'Yes... think of it as one of those... what do they call it... networking opportunities...'

I'm adamant. It's not acceptable. And our argument continues for long hours.

Slowly, they come back, the ghosts that haunted us.

As I guess I somehow knew they would, even if I was willing to believe otherwise for a while.

We argue about where to go for dinner, whom to meet or not meet for drinks, where to travel over a long weekend.

About why I like a movie you don't, or vice versa. I guess the final straw is when you come home early from work once, and find me watching porn. It's a hot, stultifying summer afternoon, and I have nothing to do. I'm passing time. But I know I cannot say this when I see your face at the door. I know this whole act will be taken personally.

You look ashen, before your features are transformed by rage. I wish you'd scream at me, say, 'What the fuck do you think you're doing?' Anything, rather than just stand there, looking at me as though I'm the most disgusting thing in the world.

I *am* the most disgusting thing in the world. I'm back to that. To feeling I am never enough, or good enough for you. That the differences between us are insurmountable, and not just when it comes to movies or vacations or whatever. And that somehow I am placed lower in this hierarchy, always.

I stop by at your place after a meeting one day, thinking this is it. I will tell you it's over.

But I walk in and find you kneeling on the floor, Muji in your arms. You are crying. Tears running down your face. The cat is shivering, and has scratches on its face and ears and, on closer inspection, a bite over its left hind leg.

'What happened?' Even though it's quite obvious.

An older cat in the area must have attacked her, and Muji, soft, gullible Muji, couldn't defend herself. You explain how

you couldn't find her anywhere that day, and only later did you hear her mewling downstairs. You searched for her all over, the garage, the storeroom cupboard, and finally found her crouched under a parked car. She wouldn't come to you for the longest time, so you had to crawl on all fours to try and catch her. It was strange, you said, for a second she turned on you too, snarling and hissing.

'She was frightened, that's all.'

But I can see it's shaken you.

I place my arm around your shoulders, I pull you close, you place your head on my chest, and my heart breaks.

'Shouldn't we get her to a vet?' you ask, and I say no, that the wounds don't appear all that bad. Muji, I assure you, will be fine. You don't seem too convinced, but agree. We feed her some of her favourite food, and allow her to rest in her favourite corner.

The next morning, though, Muji's left side is swollen like a balloon, and from the bite, whitish-yellow pus drips down her fur. When we press the swelling, more of the stuff oozes out.

'Let's go,' I say, picking up the cat basket you bought from the pet store. We place Muji inside as gently as we can, and then rush to the animal clinic. Outside, we wait agonising minutes as she's treated. Later, the vet emerges. He says they've done all they could, but we must bring the cat in every morning for the next two weeks to drain the wounds.

At home, we watch Muji crawl around on her front paws as her hind legs have been bandaged. It is pitiful.

You cry and I sit next to you feeling like I'm a million miles away.

I'm also bereft but cannot express it. I guess I'm sad for other things too. That I thought I could feel for you the way I once did, but cannot. It has passed. Despite the second chance, the restart, the new hope, we cannot be saved.

Yet I say nothing of this now or for the next fortnight, when the days are a blur of travel to and fro, from home to the clinic and back again. And hand-feeding Muji, and medicating her, and changing her bandages.

At the end of each day, you collapse into bed exhausted, and I lie next to you, listening to you breathing.

Slowly, Muji recovers, and so do your spirits. The swelling gradually lessens, the infection doesn't return, and eventually she's declared a healthy cat. You are exhilarated, and cannot stop hugging me. You feel we have done this together, and there is nothing now we cannot see through. The days resettle into normalcy. Muji and you are the same. Somehow, I think you feel we are sealed, that our lives have been welded by what has happened. Soon, somehow, I will, I must, tell you you are wrong.

THE FLORIST

How do I tell you this is not love?

It isn't and cannot be.

If I'd known, I wouldn't have walked into that pub. No, that's not true. I would've walked into that pub, and watched you, and then slipped away quietly.

This is also untrue.

I'm not the kind to think too much about anything.

I like surfing, and motorbikes, and drinking beer with my friends on weekends. I work with machines. The only books I read are self-help books. The ones about cheese or something. My parents are divorced, I'm close to my mother, I have an elder sister, and a dog at home. Once a year, I take a holiday during the summer, usually to the seaside. But I like travelling, and I will venture to unlikely places if I can afford to. When I find the one I want to marry, I will take her away and propose to her on a gondola. That's my idea of romance.

And that's really all there is to know about me.

I don't much like the city I live and work in now, filled with stone bridges. I come from the eternal city, to the south, and I miss it, but for now I cannot return. Jobs are not easy to come by these days, and I have a strong sense of responsibility.

Believe me when I say I will not forget you.

I do not love you, but I will not forget you.

How can I?

For a few days, it is true, you lifted me out of myself.

It's one of those afternoons in July, when you can really feel it's building up to the hottest time of the year. The tourists are going crazy, and so are the hawkers. Queues wind for miles outside every sightseeing spot in the city. I'm used to it now and know which streets to avoid. I park my car on a road close to the pub and walk. It's Saturday, I'm happy to be off work. I have the weekend to myself, and I've come to watch tennis at the only place in the city that's showing the match. This English pub. Or an 'English pub' as it's imagined to be, here on the continent. All wood-panelled, beer on tap, leather sofas. There aren't many people inside. Most come to this city to see art and architecture, and a couple of guys hitting a fluorescent ball over a net isn't on their agenda.

You are sitting at the bar.

In a white dress with pale blue flowers. Your feet are clad in summer sandals. Your hair falls to your shoulders. Your

arms are tanned and bare. Sitting, you appear small. Before you, a tall pint and a bowl of crisps. You have your back to me. You're watching the match intently. I cannot see your face.

At first I'm intrigued because you're the only woman here, and I wonder if you are beautiful. If you have a face I will not forget.

Then you turn to speak to the bartender.

Your cheeks are flushed, as if you've been out in the sun for too long. But your eyes are wide and bold, and dark as nights that carry promise. You glance around the pub, at the two other men watching the game, and then at me. You look a moment, and smile.

'Whom are you cheering for?'

It takes me a moment to realise you're speaking to me.

'The best man.'

You pull a face. 'So diplomatic... and boring.'

You have no idea how right you are. That's who I am. Though I'm taken aback by your forthrightness.

'Where are you from?' I cannot place you, not even from your accent.

You tell me.

'Show,' I say, and whip out my phone. It is an excuse to allow me to sit closer to you. You smell of sweat and salt, and something sharp and sweet, like peaches.

'Here.' You point at a spot on the map on-screen.

'That's very far away... you are here on holiday?'

You sip your beer and nod.

'And you're travelling on your own...?'

At this, you seem... what is the word... incensed. 'I am,' you say, 'though my parents wanted to turn this into a family holiday... but no, this is for myself and myself alone. Though, I wouldn't have minded bringing my cat.'

I'm sitting there feeling slightly awkward and confused, and you see this, I think, and laugh, 'Sorry... I don't know why I'm telling you all this... I am indeed on my own.'

'And how are you liking this city?'

'I hate it.'

I cannot help but laugh. This directness is new to me. It's also at odds with your appearance, your floral attire and flowing hair.

'Why?' I ask, even though I think I know.

'Too many tourists... too crowded... I don't even like your cathedral, all pink and white and green.'

You assume I'm from here, and I don't correct you. Oddly enough, I feel defensive about this place that isn't my own.

'You haven't given it a chance.'

'I have,' you insist, and tell me how you spent all morning walking, looking for a quiet square, an empty church, a restaurant that isn't trying to fleece you. 'It's horrible,' you conclude.

Maybe, I suggest, I could show you something that will change your mind.

Instead of backing away, suspicious, you appear interested. You have a heart as open as the sky. It is rare, and I am touched.

That, or you could be well and truly fed up of this place.

We watch another game or two, finish our beers, and leave.

At my car, you almost get into the driver's seat, because where you come from people drive on the other side. We laugh, and you slide in easily to my right.

'Where are we going?'

I say, 'Wait and see.'

We head to the river, and then slowly out of town, up wooded slopes. You tilt your head to look up, at the trees and the sky, and say it's lovely.

You are lovely.

Your dress shifts, I try not to stare at your thighs. Your throat. The neckline of your dress falls just to where the swell of your breasts begins, smooth and soft. I don't know how but I want – I must have – my mouth on them, on you.

'Oh,' you suddenly exclaim, and for a moment I wonder if you've read my thoughts and are appalled.

'I don't know your name...'

It's true. I hadn't thought to ask, and neither had you.

Solemnly, we exchange names.

'Does it make a difference?'

No, you say. It makes no difference at all.

I stop at the top of the hill. On one side there's a church, a classical white structure with wide stairs, and across from it a popular viewing point, with a curved balustrade running along the edge. It is quieter than the centre of town, but I see your face and guess it isn't quiet enough. Still, we lean against the railing, looking down at towering spires and red-tiled roofs and bridges.

'In 1966, the city was flooded by the river... and that's the most exciting thing to have happened here lately.'

You laugh, and look at me in the sunshine as though you're seeing me properly for the first time.

'What do you do?'

I tell you I work with machines. That I'm an engineer.

'What kind of engineer?'

I help make precision instruments for rockets.

Your eyes widen. 'That's amazing.'

'It's not like I go into space,' I say, laughing.

'But something of you does.'

'Yes,' I admit. 'I suppose so. I've never thought of it that way. And you?' I ask. 'What do you do?'

You tell me you are a trapeze artist.

And I take you seriously, until you begin to laugh when I ask if you're part of a circus troupe.

'Why don't you ask me what I've always wanted to be,' you say.

'All right, what have you always wanted to be?'

'An origamist.'

'A what?' I have no idea what you just said.

'An origamist. Someone who does origami.'

I feel foolish. 'What is origami?'

'The art of folding paper into shapes.'

'What kind of shapes?'

You shrug. 'Anything. Animals, birds, insects, boxes...'

'But... why?'

You look at me as though you haven't thought of that before. 'Because... I suppose... well, my school art teacher would know.'

'And what would he say?' I ask.

'Knowing him, he'd probably say it's because we're curious creatures... that we like imitating the world and seeing how we can do that in different ways...'

'And why do you like it?'

You hesitate. 'I think... because with origami you don't need anything else. You don't add paint or ink... you don't take away from it, like with sculpture... you start with a sheet of paper, and end with a sheet of paper, yet somehow... it's transformed.'

Just then there's a loud cheer behind us. Tourists have arrived by the busload and are taking pictures, waving their hats and flags in the air.

'Come,' I say. 'I'll take you somewhere else I think you'll like.'

Without a word, you follow.

This time, I drive us all the way out of the city.

I can see you take in the sudden openness of sunflower fields and lines of tall cypress, the fall of smooth unhindered sunlight. Twenty minutes later, we turn off the main road, and go up a gentle slope. At the end, beyond a car park, stands a medieval monastery.

You are delighted. Suddenly lively. There's a new energy in your voice and step.

You cannot stop saying how wonderful this is. That it's unmarked in any guidebook, unfound by prying tourists. We walk into the courtyard, striped in patterns of light and shadow. So quiet, you can hear the birds. Only a handful of monks remain, I tell you, and around us the pious silence deepens. We watch the sun grow fierce, then paler, setting in the distance, beyond the hills. You turn to me. 'Thank you.' I think you wish to kiss me. I can see it in your mouth. The way your eyes stay on my face a moment too long. But I can't be sure, so I will not try anything. Yet.

We get back in the car, and I offer to drop you off at the hostel where you're staying. For the moment, you don't mention meeting again.

'What are your plans for the evening?'

'Nothing, really,' you say.

'Here's my number...' I scribble it on a scrap of paper. 'If you feel like getting a drink, or dinner, send me a text...'

'Okay.' You slip it into your bag, not indicating whether you will get in touch.

This, though, is the most I'm willing to do. The rest is up to you.

I go home, this flat I share in the suburbs with two other people, and wait.

Hours pass and I don't hear from you. I'm about to give up, thinking I'll have a quiet evening in with a movie, when my phone beeps. You text the way you talk. In crisp complete sentences. 'Hi, shall we meet later? I've been trying to message you. I hope you get this.'

I pace my room, happy. 'Yes, pick you up at nine?'

'Okay. See you!'

I decide to take the tram into the city, so I can have more than one drink with you. Where shall I take you?

Later, I wait at the entrance of your hostel, watching young people come and go, laughing, talking in many different languages. And then you come out. Wearing a short denim skirt, black top, and strappy sandals. You've just taken a shower, and I can smell something citrusy in your hair. Like summer lemons.

I tell you that we can walk to the river, and you seem pleased.

This city is pretty at night.

The old bridge in particular, built from medieval stone, stretching across the river, its lights sparkling on the water.

'It was once lined with butchers.'

'What?'

'Butchers,' I repeat.

You laugh, saying that's hard to imagine.

We cross it leisurely. Sometimes our arms, our shoulders, touch, but we don't hold hands. Don't they say if a girl allows you to hold her hand, she will allow you to kiss her? I must be patient. The night has just begun, and nights like this are long. We walk around the cobbled stone streets. The city is exploding with revelry. People spill on to piazzas and church steps. It feels like there are only young people in the world. Something of that spirit infuses you. You appear delighted. Caught in this moment. You step close to ask me something, and I can sense in your voice and breath a recklessness.

'Let's have a drink,' I say, and you immediately agree.

I take you down to a place by the river, with tables set up on the bank. We order white wine. Street sellers walk up to us with roses. They must think we're dating, or a couple. I buy one to stop them pestering us, and it lies on the table between us like some sort of deep red promise. We drink, and drink some more. It is going to my head, this wine. And you. I lean across to take your hand, and you exclaim, looking at the rose, 'It's wilted... already, it's wilted...'

I say that's what it is. *Tristezza dei fiori*. The sadness of flowers.

You look at me, and cannot take your eyes away from mine. You repeat the words. The sadness of flowers.

After a carafe or more, we walk unsteadily back into the city, through the same winding streets. Soon enough, we find a restaurant that's still open.

'I love it,' you exclaim. 'It's one in the morning and people are still out for dinner.' You say this would never happen in the city with a river. Where it's cold and windy and everything shuts by ten. We sit under the awning and order ourselves some pizza. We talk now, easily, and you tell me about all the books that you love that have been written in my language.

'I only know one,' I confess. One that we studied in school. *Nel mezzo del cammin di nostra vita, mi ritrovai per una selva oscura, ché la diritta via era smarrita...*

You look at me with such joy, I feel almost like a fraud. I cannot be bringing you so much happiness in such little time.

We finish eating but not too much, because I think we are both filled with wine and giddy happiness, and then we walk the streets again. It is late. They are emptier now. We cross a bridge, and this time when our fingers touch we intertwine them and do not let go. Your hands are soft and slender. I want to know what the rest of you feels like. We wander, lost. I don't quite care where we're headed as long as I'm close to you and the smell of lemons.

At some point we stumble into a piazza.

'Bacchus, Bacchus,' you exclaim, pointing to a bronze statue.

'That's not Bacchus.'

'It is,' you insist. 'See, that's Bacchus holding a bunch of grapes.'

'That's Perseus with Medusa's severed head in his hand.'

We cannot stop laughing.

We time our steps to ancient cantos because it's late and the traffic lights have stopped working.

'Let's go back,' you say, 'let's go back to that place where we can see the entire city.'

And so we do. We turn our steps upwards, up a slope, a long flight of stairs. We're back to where we were earlier that afternoon. When we'd just found out each other's names. We lean against the railing. I turn to you, and we kiss.

I don't know how else to say this, but we kiss well together. I think you feel it too. Because your mouth widens and softens, the tip of your tongue free. There are others there too, in groups and couples, but we pay them no attention, nor they us. I kiss your neck. There is faint perfume behind your ears. You lift your face to the sky, to the stars. But you place your hands on my shoulders and allow me to go no further. I think the wine has rushed to our heads in torrents.

By the time almost everyone around us leaves, we are sitting on the steps. You leaning on me, my arm around you, slipping inside your top. We kiss and kiss and kiss, and go no further. And I am driven mad.

When we walk down, to the road, across the river, it is dawn. The first of the market trucks are pulling in with fresh meat and vegetables for the restaurants.

The wine may have worn off, but we are light-headed with sleeplessness. Near your hostel, we smell freshly baked bread.

'Will I see you tonight?'

You place your hand on my face in reply, and you are gone.

I don't know how I will attend work. At office, I am bleary-eyed and tired. But I can only think of you. I text you at about eleven. 'Will I see you? Come for dinner with me.'

'Yes,' you reply. 'Yes.'

When I finish, I rush home, shower and change, and drink more coffee. I pick you up in my car. You look fresh and rested, and are wearing a dress like a Monet painting. It is all shades of green, blue and white. Elegantly simple, with a plunging ruffled neck. I want only to hold you, to feel you through it.

'Where are we going?'

'You'll see...'

I take you some way out of town, to a restaurant filled only with 'locals'. Just the way you like it. 'See,' I tell you, 'even the menu isn't written in English.'

I want to feed you, to order you a three-course meal, but you are a small eater. Or maybe you are nervous. You seem a little withdrawn. But I press on. Our time is so short, I realise. Tomorrow, you are leaving and heading to the eternal city, where you will be for a week.

'Maybe I'll come see you over the weekend.' I add that I haven't been home in a while. You look happy, but something

seems to be holding you back, something in your manner is restrained. I blame it on the lack of sleep, the hangover.

We laugh about how I've struggled all day at work. You say you lazed around, and then went for a walk with a friend you'd made at the hostel. She helped you buy this dress, you say shyly.

'It's beautiful.' I mean it. You are beautiful, and I want you.

You pick at your food, and only seem interested when we are brought dessert. I show you how to dip cantucci in the sweet liqueur. I hold it up to your mouth, and you take a bite.

Later, in the car, parked outside your hostel, I taste the vin santo on your lips. You hesitate at first, but slowly I feel the restraint of the evening melt away. My hands find the ruffle around your neckline, and dip inside. You gasp but don't stop me. I hold your nipple, hard as a pebble on a beach. I place my mouth over it, and you moan, your fingers in my hair, holding me down.

'Will you come see me?'

At that moment, I am ready to take a trip into space to see you. I nod, yes, yes, yes, moving my lips to your neck. In the car, we kiss endlessly.

Over the next weekend, I drive to the eternal city.

I'm there by lunch, and meet you at a metro station outside the city centre. You are slightly more tanned. You've

been walking a lot, you tell me. You say you love it here. Your pink dress falls in soft layers to your knees. How pretty, I tell you, how pretty. On our way out of the city, I stop at a park, far from the tourist spots. We walk around. I bump into some neighbourhood friends who look at you curiously. I buy you ice cream in a little cup. A scoop of lemon, the colour of summer. And you eat daintily, licking the tip of the spoon like a cat. Then we drive out.

'Where?'

Again I don't tell you. I'm taking you to the sea. This city used to be a port a thousand years ago, and we're not too far from the coast. When we arrive, you appear thrilled, even more so than when I took you to the monastery. We park and walk to the beach, a long stretch of sand with rows of tented restaurants. We walk to the water's edge, holding hands. There is something in your eyes that terrifies me. You think this is love.

I think it is too. But I know it's short-lived. And you, I fear, don't.

I pull you away from a wave, but it splashes you and wets your dress. You laugh out loud like a child. We kiss in light that's slowly fading into deepest blue. In our ears the roar of wind and water. We stroll, and finally decide to stop at a restaurant and order wine and dinner. You can't stop touching me. And giving me kisses. We kiss above our plate of starters. Our waiter is amused and smiles, and is patient.

Tonight, it is lobster, I declare. Sitting grandly on a plate. Wrapped in foil of shiny silver. I help you cut it, breaking away the meat from the shell.

But you are distracted and excited, and you eat in quick, erratic spurts. You wave away dessert, but allow me to refill your glass.

When we stumble back out on to the beach, it has emptied. We lie on the sand, and look at the stars. You sing a song about downfalls and paper and how stars are just old light.

Then you turn to me, radiant, and tell me to teach you curses in my language. I think those kinds of words must not escape your pretty mouth, and I give you others instead. Words for beauty, and truth, and loveliness. You do not know and repeat them with ferocity, until I laugh, and you guess and push me away.

But I hold your face in my hands and kiss you, and you are soft and yielding. Then you move, and you are over me, your weight on my chest, and behind you I can see only the dark sky.

'Where shall we go after this?' you whisper.

'To a hotel?'

You make a face. For you, the idea is distasteful. Inconvenient that you should feel so, but right now I will do anything to please you. Anything, shall we say, to be in you.

'Can we go back to where you're staying?' I ask.

You shake your head. It's another hostel, you tell me, and you're in a shared dorm room.

This leaves us with little choice then. We can sneak into my house, but you must promise to be quiet. You nod solemnly.

On the way, the road dark and emptied of traffic, you fall asleep against my shoulder. I drive all the way in second gear so that I don't wake you.

At home, the dog lifts her head when she sees us, but doesn't bark. My mother is asleep. We tiptoe across to my room, where we fumble in the darkness. We fall into bed and we fuck until dawn.

The next day, we leave when my mother has stepped out of the house, as she always does on Sunday morning. We stop at a bar for breakfast, and order some coffee and a plate of pastries from the bakery. I feed you one, and you say it's delicious, but on your face I can see sadness.

Without asking, I'm quite certain it's because I'll be driving back later today. Tomorrow, I must be at work. With every passing hour, I can sense your growing attachment. But surely you can, and you must, see this for what it is.

'Why don't I come with you?' you suggest. Just for the night. And you'll take the train back tomorrow morning. You look at me with such pleading in your eyes that I don't have the heart to disagree. How could I possibly say no? Because

it's not that I wouldn't like to be with you, but that I know it's impossible.

We pick up some of your things from the hostel where you're staying, and then we drive out again into a beautiful summer evening. The sun falls long and slanting across the road, and the air is a deep, rich golden. You seem so happy by my side. I reach out and touch your knee. You turn to me and smile. How content we are to grasp at so little.

'Why did you pick this country,' I ask, 'for a holiday?'

You say it was so you could find me. And you add that you're joking, of course, but I know somewhere in there runs a little truth. Then you say that this year you turned thirty, and that you wanted to mark it in some way. 'So I chose to travel... on my own... because I wanted to learn how it is all right to journey alone...' Somewhere in you I sense, like in all of us, a deep, aching need for love. We sit in silence for a while, travelling noiselessly down the highway, locked and shut out in the car. On the radio, someone sings about a million faces passing by, how they're all the same and nothing seems to change. Who knows, who knows, the singer croons, just what the future may hold. Will it be with you?

It is horribly cheesy, but on this drive, strangely not so. I know there is no future with you. That we have met, and we will part. That it is only for the here and now, no matter how far our intimacy seems to extend into the future. I cannot

imagine how you refuse to see that. Surely it cannot be? All I can do is ignore it. But I will say this, that it lends something to the space between us. You have filled it with hope. That is the terrible thing I see in your eyes. Hope.

THE CRUSADER

WE ARE SEPARATED by a room.

The writer who inhabits it is a reclusive one; he eats his meals apart from us all, and goes for solitary walks. It's a language issue, we think, when we discuss him in the evening, when we gather in the veranda for drinks and dinner. He, I like to think, is sandwiched between desire. You and I. I don't say this, of course, not in front of the others.

When I finally kiss you, that night, when there's no frog in your room, you tell me I have a delicate face. That you noticed it the first time we met. It was late afternoon, the winter sun pale silver, and I was sitting at the veranda table. You were behind me. I looked back. You held out your hand. I stood up, smiled, and grazed your fingers with mine. I'd been there a week; you'd just arrived.

After that we didn't talk for ages.

The ones we pretend to ignore are the ones we're most aware of.

And that's what it was like the first few days. When we'd walk to the common dining area for lunch, or make ourselves breakfast or tea at our veranda kitchenette. You'd stay in your room a lot then. Everybody does when they first arrive. But we're a friendly group, the seven of us, apart from the strange writer, and I think the ice properly breaks at full moon. That evening, when it is larger than anything we city folk have seen in our lives, or at least for a long while since our childhoods perhaps. I don't remember who suggested we go outside. Could it have been you? You're like that, I notice. Impulsive. Ideas bolting from you like wild horses. I like it. It makes me imagine that, with you, anything could happen; that there will always be surprises.

So out we troop. In our slippers and shorts and pyjamas. We stay on the path a while, and then veer off to the place where they've built an outdoor performance area. It resembles a ruin, intentionally or not, I'm uncertain, but it's made of stone, and looks medieval. We sit atop the roof jutting out over the stage. I've rolled a joint, and pass it around. You take small quick puffs. The talk is loose and easy. There's a playwright, a sound artist, a translator, and most of the others are novelists. Including you, I think. I haven't asked you yet. I'm rarely shy, so I'm not sure why I'm behaving this way, like some sort of love-struck teenager. You're wearing white, and in the moonlight, the fabric glows as though lit from within. Soon, someone steps up to give us all a

performance – a few lines from Shakespeare ('To pee or not to pee', 'Get thee to a brewery'), with dramatic pauses and gestures, and they're joined for an impromptu interpretative dance. We're all in splits. Of course, the weed helps. You and I catch each other's eye while laughing. The moon rises a little higher; the trees bend in the breeze.

The next night, it is just you and I.

No one else seems up for a walk. Also, it's late, much later than usual, and this time everyone has retired to their rooms.

'But what a waste of a moon,' you say, and I declare it shall not be wasted. We walk out into the darkness. The place we're at is set within a classical dance school in the middle of nowhere. The only lights come from our building, or ones located further inside the campus. At our feet, the earth is angry red, and at night it is deep and dark as blood. We walk along the path, but do not stray from it. It feels like so much more than a walk. Up ahead, we can see the metallic glint of the gate. Beyond that lie fields, and straight rows of trees hemming the edges.

'Will it be locked?' you ask. And suddenly, somehow, your question refers to so much more than just the gate.

If it's open, I silently decide, there is hope. If it isn't, we turn back around and head back to our separate rooms, our separate lives. We walk on, our slippers crunching soil and stone and fallen leaves. And get there, our hands raised

to the bars like prisoners. We're locked in, and everything before us collapses upon itself, out of our reach. Yet, not to be defeated, you push; I help you, and something clicks. We see that the lock hasn't been snapped shut. We pull at the latch, and the gate opens. We are truant children.

'Didn't someone warn us about leopards or something?' I whisper.

'Yes.'

We giggle, stepping beyond the border. The road is lumpy with grass and tyre-ploughed mud; there's a large patch that's slushy from day-old rain. We stand just beyond the gate, the night pressing hard around us. In the grass, a streak of silver moves. We gasp and clutch each other's hands and don't let go. In the air, a heady mix of fear and excitement.

'Shall we walk on ahead?' you ask. I nod.

We follow the curve of the road, past a cluster of underbrush, and stand at the edge of a field that appears endless. The horizon merges into the blackness of the sky. We know we cannot move ahead, for now.

The days pass in joy.

Despite what I do, and what I'm working on, I'm joyful. In truth, it is long since I've felt this way, suddenly awakened and brimming with life. It is you. It is you. It is because of you. Even now, in the depths of December, spring beckons. You could say that for the first few weeks nothing happened between us, and that would be true and untrue. I cannot

keep my eyes off you. I watch you make tea. Stir your cereal. Turn the pages of your book. I talk to you, of you, incessant as a child. And you sit near me on the cane sofa. You pass by close as a whisper in the corridor, the veranda. When we wish each other good night, it is with longing. There's no other way to say it. Once, I hear you scream, and I rush out from my room and go to your door. The translator is also there. There's a frog in your room. It's tiny, but you hate frogs. You're pointing to the corner. We both shoo it out, stamping our feet, clapping our hands, laughing. We tease you; you're sweetly embarrassed. We leave, but I linger at the door and look back at you, at your room, which smells of you and something citrusy.

Then I wish for a frog to be in your room every night.

I wish to be the frog in your room.

Finally, I ask you what it is that you're working on at this residency. It's a cool, breezy afternoon, quiet as a church, and we're sitting with cups of tea in the veranda. I don't know where everyone else is; they aren't here and I hope it stays that way.

You say you're here because of your workplace, a book house, that you're working on putting together their archives, and this place seemed perfect.

Although you wish you were involved in a more... personal project.

'Like what?'

'Like... I don't know... writing a book.'

'About what?'

You make a funny face before you say, 'Love.'

I say that definitely hasn't been done before.

You laugh. 'Something epic.'

Yes, epic love, that too is new.

You say you can't convince me, of course – not like this – but maybe one day you'll write the book, and I'll read it and know what you mean.

'Will I be in it?'

'Everyone I loved, or love, will be in it.'

And you smile, at all sorts of remembrances I'm sure, and I grow jealous of your memories because those are times in your life I will never be a part of, and I imagine them large and exuberant in your head.

'Oh,' I ask slyly, 'and how many times have you been in love?'

You sip your tea, some strange kind, green, with bits of roasted rice, and shrug.

'How does one know? It could be love every time. People think it's hard, that it's the most difficult thing in the world... but it's easy to love.'

My heart constricts, expands. I'm envious of whoever the person is, or the people are, who have been the recipients of your affection. I'm also glad, because you are capable of love.

Maybe you can love me.

'Which was your longest?'

You gaze outside, at nothing in particular. 'Five days...'

I exclaim, 'Is that true? How so? Have you never been in a long relationship?'

For years, you reply, with a musician. Or at least someone you hope is now a musician. But five days can sometimes feel like a lifetime.

I think about our almost-month here, and say it's true.

'Where did you meet him? When?'

'A few years ago... while I was on holiday... so obviously, eventually I had to leave...'

You stay silent; you are elsewhere. The breeze pushes your hair away from your neck, and I long to touch it, to run my finger down the line of your throat.

'Why him?' I want to know and I don't want to know.

You take a moment to answer. 'Thinking about it now, I don't know if it was him in particular... Sometimes what's external also plays a part, don't you think?'

I say I'm not sure I understand.

'What I mean is, we feel it's the right time to be in love... the right age... the right season... the right whatever... and the person is incidental.'

'So you're saying the greatest love of your life could've been... anyone?'

'Yes.' You laugh, and sip your tea. 'I suppose that's not entirely true... He was nice, and very cute... and at that moment, very right...'

And I smile, but somewhere a sting of jealousy burns deep and flame-bright.

'And you?' you ask. 'What do you do?'

I tell you I work in that most lonesome of vocations.

'You're... a poet?'

'Worse. I publish poetry.'

'Oh dear.'

We laugh for a moment, before you ask me why.

This is not usually the first thing people ask. They say it's wonderful, or noble, or amazing.

I tell you that my father was a poet. Well, he was also a professor, but a poet always. He wrote in a language other than English, and after he died, since there was no one else to do it, I translated his work, and found no one to publish it.

So I quit my job as a journalist – 'I was shit at it anyway' – and set up an independent publishing house. My publishing house, I tell you, is run mostly on love and fresh air, and foreign funding. And unbelievably, we're still here, somehow unsinking.

'It must be hard,' you say simply.

It is, but nobody has said that to me either.

'So now?'

So now I'm putting together an anthology.

'What kind of anthology?'

I'm almost embarrassed to say, because I'm hoping to impress you, just a little. 'One of those "celebrate a decade of verse" anthologies...'

'You've been doing this for ten years?'

I nod, and at this point, I can't not admit this. 'We. We have...'

'You and...?'

'My wife.'

'Oh.' Your tone is inscrutable.

How do I tell you what it really is? I don't know where to begin.

'How long have you been married?'

My tea is cold and tasteless. 'Seventeen years.'

'You both must have been so young.'

'Yes,' I say, 'several lifetimes ago.'

'How does it feel?' you ask.

'What do you mean?'

'To be with someone... for so long...'

I think about how five days could be a lifetime, a month too. Seventeen years is short in comparison. What do I want to say? Eventually I settle on the truth.

'We are good... companions.'

Your face is cryptic. I want to take your hand, but your fingers are wrapped tightly around your empty cup, as though by some miracle it's keeping them warm.

That night there is no frog in your room, but you ask me to check anyway. No frogs. No lizards.

Then we stand in the centre, looking into each other's faces.

'Do you think something might have happened if...'

I finish for you. 'I wasn't married?'

You nod.

'What do you think?'

We're standing so close together, I can feel your breath on my face.

'I don't know...' For the first time, I hear a trace of nervousness in your voice and this is what makes me lean in and kiss you. You take my face in your hands. When we part, we are quiet. The world conspires to silence. Outside, the crickets have stopped. The dogs are away. The wind is quiet. For miles, there is only the sound of our breathing. You trace my jawline with your fingers, and tell me I have a delicate face.

We kiss again. This time more urgently. My hands travel down your back, but that is when you step away.

'Okay,' you whisper, 'you should go...'

I am slain. But I say goodnight, and leave. I lie awake all night wondering if this will happen again. If there will be more. I think about the gate, and how it felt under our hands. How it clicked open, and allowed us outside.

The next day, there is newness, and a frisson, of something that hasn't quite yet solidified. The air is ripe with endless possibilities. When we step out of our rooms, even breakfast is an adventure. Yet daylight, as it must, keeps us apart. Mostly. I manage to sneak into your room like a schoolboy after lunch and we lie on the bed. We do not undress, or go

beyond chaste kisses. There is the night for that, and I can hardly contain myself. The day, though, seems terribly long. The hours mock us by stretching and passing slowly. You go for a walk in the late afternoon, with the translator and the sound artist. I am sitting in the veranda working, and I can see the three of you receding as you walk across the field. Go, go, I think to myself, and come back with twilight in your hands.

When you return, your shoes are dusty red, from the soil that is the colour of fire. I have cooked you dinner. Well, I have cooked dinner for everyone. A country chicken curry that will be eaten with pasty local grain. This too is heavy and earth-red, and steamed and rolled into a ball that we pick and mash and mix with gravy. You are hungry; you eat with your hands, but like someone who isn't used to it. What else can those hands do?

I am distracted, and now irritated by the never-ending day. People are in the mood to linger. Alcohol is brought out; drinks are poured. How I would have liked everyone to say they were suddenly tired, and wish each other goodnight, and retire. But they don't. There is chatter, and music, and I think I shall burst in rage. In anticipation. For a second I think nothing will happen tonight. That we must wait again through the day tomorrow. And if we do, I shall die.

Around midnight though, the group thins. People start wandering back to their rooms. We are left, along with the

playwright and the translator. Insects circle the lights. A toad hops out from under the sink, giving you a fright. I am calmer. Knowing that there will be time for us to be together.

Finally, we all stand up to leave. You give me a look. And I understand. We'll go to our separate rooms, and then I'll join you.

I wait an impatient five minutes in the dark, on my own bed, and then dart down to your door. You are lying in bed, wearing what you wore that full moon night. White. Everything narrows to our kiss. The day has happened only to lead us here, to this moment. You slide your hands across my chest, my shoulder, my back. I kiss your neck, and you moan softly. I am on top of you, but trying to keep my weight light. I do not want to scare you, or seem too eager. Soon, I am tugging off my shirt. You keep yours on. Except I slowly undo the top buttons and slide my mouth lower. I see the edge of your bra, white and lacy, and I want to weep. I push it aside slowly with my tongue, and when my mouth finds your nipple, you sigh. I cannot, cannot get enough of you. But I'm afraid to rush. So I take deep breaths, and try and slow down. You seem in no hurry. I take off my pyjamas and am naked.

'Pull it,' I whisper, as your fingers grasp the hair on my chest. And it hurts. And it is exquisite. You have slipped your top off and your bra.

You are so beautiful.

I haven't taken things this slow since I was a teenager and sex was out of the question. It is a slow burn. Something I haven't done in a long time. Sex is usually always performed in a hurry. The prelude breathless and hasty, so we can get to the act quickly. And it is over quickly too. Now, though, I don't know where we are heading. You keep me guessing. You relish the kissing, the sliding of skin on skin, the fingers finding crevices and lines, the slow undressing.

At some point, my hands glide over your stomach, and lower to the top of your waistline. Grazing the elastic that hugs you. You place a hand gently on mine.

'We can't...'

'What?' I'm not sure I'm hearing right.

'Tonight... I mean not tonight...'

Before I can help myself, I ask why. I shouldn't have. It is not right.

But you don't seem perturbed. You tell me you have your period.

I don't mind, I mutter into your hair, your ear. I really don't.

'But I do.'

I say I understand, and I kiss you deeply, my hand sliding back up. You can feel me though, I know you can, digging into your thigh. And I can't help but rub myself against you, slowly, as though I'm moving in you. You wet your palm and place your hand on me. For a moment, I cannot breathe. All

life is knocked out of me. You move your fingers, slippery with spit, and cup me in your palm. I throw my head back and moan. I cannot stop myself, even in these quiet quarters. In the darkness, the world has narrowed to this bed. Then you make me lie down, and move on top, and... I can hardly believe it... move lower. There has been sex with many other women, on travel for work, and conferences, and drunken office parties, but a long time since this. Your mouth is warm and smooth and magic and takes me to the end and back to the top, to the end, and back to the top. And faster. Your fingers massaging along with your lips in some infinite pattern of desire.

It doesn't take me long, and I feel like the room fills with my breathing, and love, and the smell of you and me and dampness.

Later, you lie with your head on my chest. My arm around you. It isn't yet dawn, but it must be close. We are pleasantly tired, but sleepless. I may never sleep again. You have your clothes on; I am naked.

I run my fingers down your face, your shoulder, your arm.

'When was your first time?' I ask.

I think I hear you wrong, because you mumble something about a kitchen stool. 'What?'

You turn up to me. 'Nothing.'

'It's okay if you don't want to tell me...' It isn't; I desperately want to know.

'No, it's nothing like that...' You'd almost finished university, there was this boy, in your room.

A sharp pain, no blood. It was most... unremarkable.

'And yours?'

My first time was with a man, I reply.

'Oh?'

I like the small drama this creates. 'Yes, my father's colleague... an English professor... I was young, he was much older...'

'And then you got married soon after?'

'And then I got married soon after.'

'You haven't always been... faithful?'

When I stay silent, you apologise.

I take your hand in my face. 'You never have to say sorry.'

I kiss you again and again. You taste of me.

'My wife and I stopped sleeping together... I don't know how long ago... and now, well, like I said... we're companions...'

I lie back, looking up into pale darkness; I can see the outline of the fan, the wooden beams running across the ceiling.

'Does she know?'

'I think so... I don't know...'

You place your hand on my cheek, like you did when you said it was delicate. 'If you've been with other people... why do you still stay married?'

For a long while, I am silent. The question is a knife in my stomach, my heart. I think you know this and wait for me to answer, but I don't.

'Years ago,' you say, breaking the silence, 'I asked someone else the same question... an older man, a married man...'

'And what did he say?'

You turn to me, your eyes filled, I think, with pity. It kills me.

'He said he wasn't the kind of person to leave... and you know what that means, don't you?'

'What?'

'That he would always be the one to be left.'

'I was like that too, you know...' you continue, 'A "leavee", if there's such a word, not a leaver... but not any more, I like to think...'

I turn to you and ask, 'What happens when you leave people?'

You hesitate for the briefest moment. 'It allows you both to grow.'

These words too are knives, and I am cut open and illuminated at the same time.

When it comes to my wife, I want to tell you that I never wished to be the cause of pain, that that would make me a bad person. That I would judge me, and judge me so harsh it would kill me. Yet I know, I know I do it anyway. Loathe myself for what I end up doing, and not doing.

Maybe because you sense the mood spiralling, you kiss me gently on my neck, then harder, to leave a little mark. I do that on your breast. Lower. To show that somehow, at least while it lasts, you are mine. And then, like the memory of me, it will fade.

'Are you sad?'

I nod.

'Why?'

I can hardly bring myself to say it. That I'm happy, and that in this, also, is our end.

'It's like arriving at an airport, isn't it?' I begin. 'And already imagining your departure from the place... It's already embedded. We're always arriving and leaving at the same time.'

It is unbearable. We hold each other as though for the last time. But it isn't. It cannot be, I tell myself. Eventually, exhausted, we fall asleep.

But I'm fitful. I'm so afraid I will snore, or leave you with too little space, or crush your arm, that I awake, it seems, every few minutes. Soon, I can see white light pushing its way through the shutters. It falls gently on your face. When I can see the curve of your cheek, the sweep of your forehead, the outline of you clearly, I know I must go.

I open the door. It is dawn.

I meet the writer in the corridor. We wish each other good morning as though it's the most normal thing in the world, and continue on our way. He on his walk, and I to my room.

THE LIGHTHOUSE KEEPER

THE NIGHT WE decide to marry, we're drinking cheap (but organic) corner shop wine.

It's disgusting. So disgusting that we quaff down the first few glasses so the rest don't taste as bad.

We're sitting in your room, your small room, in this city with a river, which is full of buildings with small rooms. You told me much had changed since you were here last, studying, but not this.

'And when was that?' I ask.

'Almost ten years ago.'

This time, you're not here to study.

The foreign cultural institute you're attached to back in your country has sent you on an exchange visit to their office for a year. You were happy about it, you tell me, until you realised how expensive everything is here, and worse, how cold it gets when winter sets in.

So here we are, with the heating turned up, the bottle emptying, and talk freely flowing.

I admit this is all quite new for me.

How time is so easy and seems to unfurl endlessly before you. I'd never met anyone for whom it doesn't seem to matter where the hands on the watch are placed, what shape the numbers take on a digital clock. For me, when all my life I've had to account for my hours, this is like coming upon a secret oasis somewhere in the desert, where the flowers are perpetually in bloom.

You are like that.

With you my days and nights are... looser. Less like tightly wound springs.

How lucky it is that we met at the beginning of your stint here.

Someone you knew who knew someone who knew me. We were invited to dinner, and we cooked together. The two of us sitting at the table, me slicing cherry tomatoes, you drinking an unhurried glass of wine. Me with my carefully measured quantities. You with your 'a pinch of this' and 'a handful of that'. A few weeks later, we met at a concert. We went along with some friends. We chatted easily on our way home. It struck me that I liked talking to you. Another time, a few of us attended a cheap (and terrible) stand-up comedy show, and then headed out for dinner. Korean. It was a first for me, and somehow it seemed appropriate that I should try all these new things with you. Then you and I went to

your favourite Japanese restaurant, where plates came to us on a conveyor belt. That too was a whole different world. How much we talked, about where you came from, and where I did. How different our lives, now how irrevocably intertwined.

You told me you weren't with anyone. Neither was I.

And when we talked about past loves, we were candid. I'd been with someone for seven years, but we'd broken up when I told her that I felt I was on a journey of discovery I had to make on my own.

'What kind of journey?'

And I told you all, about the confusion, the attraction, the guilt. I thought I was a freak.

You said softly, 'There's no such thing.'

You are my space of no judgement. With you, I am safe.

You told me about a musician. Someone you couldn't bring yourself to leave. An older man or two.

'Were they married?'

'No.'

'What about one-night stands?'

You shook your head.

'You?' you asked quickly.

I laughed. 'Once, when I was sixteen, and on a school trip to Canada.' I don't remember her name, but I do remember she was skinny with long braided hair.

'Do all the things I tell you... discomfort you?' I wanted to say 'disgust'.

'Not at all.' Your eyes were filled with kindness. And I kissed you, and kissed you some more.

Sometimes, I take a deep breath because I cannot believe we are so lucky to have found each other in a vast, ever-expanding universe. You are beautiful, and talented, and from somewhere I can only imagine. A place I've only read about, or seen on screen.

That night, despite the wine, you seem subdued.

You are silent, looking out of the window, on to roofs and chimneys darkened by evening. I panic.

I don't want you to slide into this mood, so I make little jokes and play the clown.

My shenanigans make you laugh and lift your mood a little. Then we lie in bed, close and quiet.

'What is it?' I ask. 'What's troubling you?'

You hesitate, and then tell me in a torrent, as though it's been building in your head for days, like a rain cloud. You say you don't wish to get into anything that you must abandon in a few months, when you leave the city. That it isn't worth the pain and the heartache. You are tired of loss. And for me, you tell me, you would have liked to stay on here, but that in these times it's impossible to find a job for which you could get a visa. I don't think I've ever had to apply for one, so I find it quite confusing, but you explain it to me patiently, and say this is why it's best we part.

'What else can we do?' I'm desperate now, things weren't meant to fall apart so quickly.

'Nothing.'

'There must be something,' I insist.

'We could get married,' you joke.

'Let's.'

'You might want to think about this...'

I say I have.

Instead of rearing up in alarm, you behave as though I've asked if you'd like another glass of wine.

'Okay.'

We do not, as you say, buy into the bullshit of it all, this institution of marriage, progressives that we are, but it will keep us in the same place, and it seems like a bold, impulsive move – all the things I have never been, really.

I'm from across the channel, from the continent, further to the south, a small town in the mountains. My parents moved there from a poor part of the country when they were young and strove to be 'successful'. It is the story of all immigrants.

And so we had to be successful too, my younger brother and I. All the time. It was the only way we felt we deserved our parents' love. We had to earn it. With each good grade and goal scored, with each lap finished and won, with every exam topped.

Love became performance.

And for you, I'm ready to do my best.

Like, for example, when you tell me shyly that you're trying to work on your first book.

I'm so proud. It's going to be a great success, I tell you. I want to be sure I tell you the right things at the right time. (It won't happen always, I know, I'm not stupid. But I'll try.)

Now that you're here with me, and will stay with me, it's the least I can do.

To get to know each other better, we move in together, into this studio apartment in a building on a slope. We are opposite a dance school for children, and during the day there is music, and ballerinas, and I feel we couldn't have chosen a better place to begin our lives together. It's artistic enough, I hope, for you.

It's not something I know much about.

There hasn't been much time in my life to develop an... aesthetic, I think they call it.

You have that in abundance. The clothes you wear, the way you arrange a room, the odd bits you've collected from here and there coming together in some kind of chaotic, lovely symphony. You're older than me by five years. Maybe that has something to do with it.

Mostly I've been studying. (I think you like that about me.) Working on my PhD, ferreting around in my academic world like a mouse. That's what you call me. I say I look like

a mouse too, and you say no, that's not true. You run your hands over my arms, my chest.

I run a bit, and work out, and that keeps me in shape. From the looks of it, I think you appreciate it.

So here we are in our house.

Who'd think life could be so wild and full of surprises?

It's hard to believe that soon we'll share so much more than just the space in this room.

We'll be linked, inextricably, forever. Although we've discussed it, of course, and we're doing this for all sorts of reasons. We're showing a big middle finger to a country where you can remain if you have a job but not if you fall in love. That's what it is. A giant fuck you. People will always find ways to be together, we declare, and borders cannot stop them. I'm glad we agree on things like that. I think it's important. Meanwhile, we cook for each other. Me, some meaty dishes with sauce and herbs and things, and you try your hand at various exotic fare – some Korean seafood pancakes that turn out thick and lumpy (but I eat them and say they're delicious), a pizza we bake in the microwave. You like your drink, so we always come home from the supermarket with wine, or beer, and recently you've developed a fondness for cider. Pear cider in particular. I try to like it too.

We're keeping it small, this wedding thing. We don't want to mark it with anything more than a quiet day with a few

friends. My family will come in, and so will yours. Also, we don't really have the money for something grand. Although even if we did, we wouldn't. It's just not the sort of thing we'd do.

You make the invitations by hand, with paper cut-outs, and ribbon, and paints.

I find it terribly sweet, what you do.

This is our summer of much love.

We read, and write, and walk around the city. We like eating nice meals out, dropping by a pub for a pint. You like visiting exhibitions and art shows, and I don't want to upset or disappoint you by saying I don't care for them very much. Or at all. So I accompany you.

'What did you think?' you'll ask as we step out of the theatre or the gallery or the museum, and I feel some pressure to be clever and armed with the right opinion. But I know it makes you happy to be 'cultural' like this, so I try. And I think mostly I get it right, because you seem pleased. Sometimes when I say I haven't really understood something (I think sometimes you forget our cultural backgrounds are worlds apart), a look of annoyance crosses your face. You are terribly impatient, my love. I wish you'd be gentler on me sometimes.

Just like when you say, 'We don't read the same kinds of books,' and I sense in that a whole world of judgement. Silent, unspoken judgement is the harshest kind.

In these times, I do find it hard.

Old feelings come up. Mostly of unworthiness.

I try and battle my way out, saying I read other things, and doesn't that matter? Aren't we more enriched because our bookshelves are so varied? Wouldn't it be boring to read the same books? But I don't insist. I don't want to hurt you. I guess I'm watchful.

And attentive.

You like that, I can sense it.

When I carry your luggage into the train, and hold the door open for you, and ask if there's anything you'd like to eat or drink, or whether you're cold and wish to wear my jacket, and if you're comfortable. Which is why I also like getting you gifts. A sweet pastry, a dozen fresh kiwis, a pair of gloves with which you can still use your touchscreen phone, a membership to an art museum so that you can attend shows free for a year, a singing class. These are my gestures, which I hope show you how appreciative I am. I like you to know that I think of you when I'm away from you.

'Don't spend so much on me,' you'll say.

Which is funny because the one thing you don't like talking about is money.

This is awkward.

But perhaps after we're married this will change, because then everything we own individually will become ours.

Our wedding day comes and goes.

Simple, just as we wished. A no-nonsense ceremony, a lunch, a toast. The weather held, the sun shone until late in the evening, sliding across the city in long fingers. Lovely and autumnal, I heard you say. You like words like that. Autumnal.

After this there is a lull.

And while I have tonnes of work to catch up on, you find yourself with nothing much to do.

You read, you are restless. You cannot write. You're struggling with your book.

I'm worried. But I don't show it. What if one morning you wake up and say, 'This is not for me, I'm leaving'?

So I try and mollify you. There's an art show somewhere you wish to attend, and I concede to accompanying you even though I'm interested in it as much as I am in dung beetles. But I try keeping you happy.

You get a job too, in an office nearby. Admin stuff like updating a database and sealing envelopes. I think you will die of boredom. It makes my heart ache to see you leave every morning. Hat, coat, and gloves on, because it's freezing now. You don't complain, but of course how can this be what anyone wants? It's hard in this city with a river, because the rents are steep (even for small rooms), and with only my stipend coming in. We cannot go on holiday, even after our wedding, or eat out as often as we like, or attend shows.

It makes me feel I'm not enough for you.

In a few months, we decide to move out to another city, this time by the sea. It's not far, and it's beautiful and, more importantly, less expensive. I can come in once a week to teach my classes and meet my supervisors. You can stay home and write, I declare.

I think it's like a present to you on my part, this gesture. No more silly office admin jobs. You are an artist. Your fingers are for finer things than stamps and envelopes. You acquiesce. And we move and set up house, small but charming, all wooden floors and fireplace. We pass our winter here quite happily. We discover a love for bingeing on movies, and I'm getting to like fish and seafood, though not as much as you do. We discover a tea shop, where we play Scrabble and cards. We have quiet evenings in. We drink a pint or two with acquaintances.

And then one day you ask me, 'Don't you think we're living a life of retirement?'

I'm shattered. And pissed off.

I've given you a house, and everything you could possibly want in it. I don't understand.

'What do you mean?' I ask.

'Just that,' you struggle to reply, 'we live like old people.'

But I mustn't show you my anger, or my hurt, because you are being honest with me.

'I see what you mean,' I say, even though I don't, but I try. I have never lived a life of hedonism. I wonder about you. 'What would you like to do?'

You're unable to answer, and seem exasperated. I begin to say, 'I know we don't know many people here, in this city by the sea, and that...'

'There's not much to do either, is there?'

I thought we kept ourselves busy, with our long, long walks along the promenade every evening.

'Let's go somewhere,' you say. And this becomes, I notice, a recurring request. Let's go somewhere, anywhere, to get out of this rut. We cannot afford it, I want to shout, but I don't, and I ask where you'd like to go.

You mention some lovely, sloping island surrounded by the brilliant blue of the Mediterranean.

'Yes,' I say. 'Well, we cannot right now...'

'Oh, don't be so pragmatic.' You sound exhausted. 'Just say yes! And let's imagine how it would be to walk those winding alleyways that open out to the sea.'

I'm confused by you. Do you mean what you say? Are you on some flight of fantasy?

This happens quite often.

You'll suddenly look up, and proclaim you want to go somewhere, the city of this, the city of that, a country here, a country there. Please. And I say cautiously that we have to plan it properly, because I do not wish to make promises I cannot keep, and that annoys you. 'You have no adventurous bone in you,' you complain, and that hurts me. I'm an adventurer in my own way. For example, before I met you, I

was dating men who liked to dress up as women, and people who did not ascribe to themselves a gender. You know this, of course, because I've told you, but you seem to think there is only one way to be an adventurer: yours. Still, I don't want to upset you.

So I learn, as you put it, to play along. But I don't understand why you indulge in this invented escape, or what pleasure it brings. What happiness can lie in something entirely imaginary?

Next time you say let's go here, or there, I pretend gleefully to agree.

When you start writing, you are calmer.

Then I too enjoy some days of uninterrupted work, which is rare, and what I desperately need, because how else will I finish this colossal project of a PhD? I'm working and earning and teaching, and trying to keep you happy, but there are demands that crop up frequently.

A meal out, a pint, a trip to the city with a river, a show. And I go. You are lovely but selfish. Is that the word? Or self-centred? But then you tell me you have sleepless nights sometimes. That you lie on the couch in the living room because you don't want to wake me, and you see dawn, and hear the sounds of morning, and then my heart breaks again.

You moved here for me.

I must be there for you.

So we do make these trips sometimes. I put away some money from my stipend, or dip into our savings, and we rent a car, and it's all worth it, I think, just to see the look on your face when we drive out of the city and hit the motorway and there is a sense of speed and wildness around us. We visit your friends in the countryside, the ones you said you once spent a summer with and they took you to a pebbly beach. We stay with them in their house with corridors lined with books, and they love that you are writing. They welcome me, and treat me as part of the family. We sit around the dining table and talk for hours. You ask about some student who was staying in the house when you were here last time. I see that you change with people around you. You blossom. You laugh more. Even though I try to make you laugh in our flat. I do silly dances, and mimic and mime. I've always loved to perform to make people happy. My mother used to say I'd be wonderful on stage, but what's the point in saying that when they only pushed me towards a 'safe' career and lucrative jobs. Finance. Economics. Law. My younger brother wanted to be a truck driver, he'd once declared, and travel across the continent. Our parents laughed it off, but now I don't see why. He might have been happier as a truck driver rather than as some financial consultant who works like a dog. And surely that's what's important. They even think this PhD is a waste of time. Academics don't make money, or not enough money. But how much is enough money?

You still don't like to talk about it.

I've tried to involve you in the running of the household. You know, paying the bills, keeping accounts, but you pretend to be interested and concerned and then wander off. You like playing the part of the flighty artist, I think. It's a part you play well. And it's also convenient because it means you don't have to deal with the... dirty laundry, I think they call it? The boring house stuff. You can focus on fairy lights, and framing pictures, and collecting odd things from antique stores. A green bottle, a red lantern, a glass candleholder. I think it brings you joy, so I allow you to, though we can barely afford it. But how would you know?

After we've been in the city by the sea for almost two years, we decide to move again.

Not to anywhere nearby, but across the world, where you come from, your home country. I'm confused by my motives. I don't think I'm doing this only for you, but I think that plays a large part. For our survival. Also, isn't this how 'let's go somewhere' finally becomes real? You are excited, I think, and nervous. I'm worried. But I busy myself with logistics, with the planning and plotting. It is fine. It will be fine. We dismantle our home, the pictures, and curtains, and books, and linen. They all get packed into cardboard boxes or are given away. In the air, there is a sense of adventure, despite the stress of shifting.

It's the deciding that's most difficult. Should we keep this? Should this stay? Everything must be weighed. Some things we cannot part from. Our books are the heaviest of all. Our clothes we cull. We will set up house elsewhere. It will be terrifically exciting. In the midst of all this, I cannot work, but I try not to panic. There will be time, I tell myself, there will be time. In this year or so, we have lived beyond our means, but you don't know that, and I'm hoping we can settle more comfortably where we will be. It will be cheaper. I will get a job. Perhaps you will too. You have contacts, you say chirpily, it won't be difficult, and I'd like to trust you.

Sometimes I'm not so attentive any more, because it's hard to be forever vigilant. We have fought also. And I have walked out the door and then returned shamefaced. They are about silly things, our fights. Usually, when I finally have an outburst about going to the pub the hundredth time that week, or when you come up with another hare-brained fantasy escape plan. But they scare me, and I find I must apologise over and over. I think this confuses you, but I don't know what else to do. All this will go away when we're elsewhere, I'm sure.

Sometimes I find it hard to remember what it was like at the beginning.

When we arrive in your homeland, we stay with your parents.

This doesn't please you – it's the house where your grandparents brought you up when your mother and father

were away ('all the time,' you tell me), and you've never quite bridged that gap – but we have no choice. I think you're only pleased to see the cat, a striped, cloudy grey creature named Muji, you told me you rescued a few years ago. You brought her here before you left for your office trip abroad. She is fat and cuddly and affectionate, and you are delighted to be reunited, but it's not enough to make you want to stay. 'We'll be here a few weeks... a month... and then leave,' you tell me.

Then you injure yourself.

It is almost immediate. We have barely had any time to recover, or gather ourselves. And so, instead of going forth, and finding jobs, and searching for houses to live in, we are stuck.

I'm the caregiver. You're the receiver.

Because you can barely move.

It's your back.

Something has slipped out of alignment and causes you immense pain. You must rest, and rest some more. And that is exhausting, for you, for me. I must negotiate a new place, new people, my pending PhD, and you not there and whole. I will do this for you, for us, but it is gnawing away at me.

What if I don't find a job here?

What if I can never go back to my own country? Will they take me back there after years here?

I cannot believe these questions are coming up now. They must be pushed away. You must be well. And slowly, you do

recover. I try to keep you busy but there is little to distract us in this small town. We take walks, visit cafés and tea shops, we attend the odd literary meet, and sometimes we meet up with one of your old acquaintances.

Then, out of nowhere, you fall ill with a chest infection. It is relentless.

You move to another room which is warmer, upstairs, and I'm alone in the guest room, downstairs. I am alone.

You cough and cannot breathe, you sound different, you are different.

We have not slept together in months but this is not new. It has become a task, I think, to do so. It never used to be. I remember our summer of love, but now onwards to illness, and exhaustion, and seeming non-recovery.

Finally, when the year turns new, we leave your parents' house.

You seem happier though, as am I. There is relief at not being bound to the bed, the room, this small town in the east of the country. And for you, to them.

We wander city to city, trying to make each one our home. We start out with tremendous enthusiasm, with love, but for some reason or the other we fail. Nothing is right for you. I don't know what you want. I just need a place where I can be steady and calm. This is making me nervous, like I'm constantly tossing about on a stormy sea. It is also expensive,

I want to tell you, but I think this might be an inappropriate time to bring up money.

Our dreams of elsewhere are fading.

So we end up – and this distresses you so much – going back to live with your parents, because we haven't found a roof to rent.

Or jobs.

This is tearing us apart.

It's unstitching us.

I cannot hold, and I cannot be attentive or vigilant any more.

I must travel back to submit my thesis. Somehow, I have cobbled it together in these past few months. And I will be away. You will join me later, you say, but before that you say you are leaving too.

For the city without a river.

You call it your city of eternal return, because you flee and come back, and flee and come back again. This time it's for something you've been invited to, a festival of some sort, to speak of books, the one you've just written, the one that will be published soon. They will put you up in a hotel, and I think you seem relieved to be free of me.

Perhaps this will be a good occasion for us to spend some time apart, to revaluate and reassess, because how much longer can this go on? And how much more can I keep giving?

I feel it has been like this for too long. Right from the beginning. I must make you happy. I must earn your love by always doing, saying, the things you want me to.

But look at how it has killed me.

I'm so tired, my love. You have taken and taken, my blood and soul, and all of me, until there will be nothing left. We are always apart now, even in the same room, no matter how small.

THE SAILOR

WE'RE BOTH AESTHETES, you and I.

Which is why we fuck so well. It looks so pretty, the yellow blindfold across your face. I take a picture; you don't know. I like taking pictures of my women when they're naked, when they aren't aware I'm doing so, else, immediately, it's lost. The nakedness. No, they don't throw on clothes, but something far more concealing. The knowledge that they're being watched. It's an immediate performance. Same thing in bed. Those postures, and moans, and grimaces on their faces straight out of porn flicks. Which is why I like to choke them a little. Place my hands around their dainty throats and tighten my grip. When it's tight enough, for long enough, the posturing drops. Something passes over their faces that's real. You do it too, you prissy thing straight out of some Victorian convent school. It makes me want you to behave badly, to drop the politeness.

And sometimes, with me, you do.

I know you best, the darkness behind your lovely elegant ways.

They threw you out of that hotel, which is how you came to stay. No, you threw yourself out, you said, because the organisers had made a mistake and double-booked, and expected you to share your room with a stranger. 'A lady writer,' they said, as though that made it okay. 'Cheapskate bastards,' you called them. You had no place to go; I had an extra room, except we didn't use it.

'Why are you here?' I asked.

'I'm fleeing.'

'Apart from that?'

You were attending some cultural festival.

'And why isn't he here? The one you're married to.'

You didn't reply.

'Are you leaving him?'

You took a moment too long to answer.

'You know,' I said. 'You already know, and so does he.'

It's the only time I'll say it, but I'm so much older than you, and I know now that these things – these driftings apart – are sensed without a word exchanged. We are telepathic. Sensitive as seismometers to the shift and shuffle of feelings.

You aren't new to me. I've known you a few years.

I met you when I was dating someone else. And we

sat in the same room. Some writer who had invited us for dinner to his small, stuffy apartment. It was depressing. Luckily, we were high by then, and I remember you in a white dress, white like summer and wild flowers and sea birds. You, sitting there, so untouched, like some virgin convent schoolgirl.

You told me you worked at a book house, some foreign cultural institute, that you'd been there a while, and could do what you do with your eyes closed, in your sleep.

'What else do you do in your sleep?' I wanted to ask. I wanted to bite your lip.

How inappropriate. I'm a dirty lecherous old man.

And then there was something else, a meeting elsewhere. I'm not good with details.

I remember you saying you'd like to write someday, perhaps.

I didn't ask why, because I understood. Then I asked what you would do otherwise?

You said you'd like to be an origamist.

Why don't you?

'I don't know if I have enough paper.'

After that we were fish in a stream, slipping past each other occasionally. An event here or there, a reading. You were always polite, and happy to see me. I was too. I didn't think

that one day I would fuck you (but I kept it in mind). Not so long ago, I met you with the one you married and you seemed happy, and I thought I was an asshole. You'd just moved back to the country, to the small town in the east, I attended a literary event there that no one else had been invited to, and I made a speech, and no one laughed at the funny bits apart from you two, and I was so thankful we went and got some wine, and it turned into a long evening, and we drank again the next day, and the next, until I left.

And then the next time I meet you, a few months later, in the city without a river, you are different. No less happy, I think, I cannot tell. And then they throw you out of that hotel. All that happens.

So you come across to mine, and I know you like the bareness of my place, its open floors, the one armchair, the bookcases, the shelf of unusual musical instruments. You notice the mirror in the bedroom, its position on the wall opposite the foot of the bed. What it would reflect. And I'm already thinking of you in it. I wonder if you too will pose for me and the mirror and yourself, and when we sleep together, I find you do. I'm a little disappointed, but I haven't ever been with a woman – and there have been many – who didn't. Except maybe my wife, and she's gone.

I make some tea; some light herbal concoction, because you don't drink coffee. Soon, that too will change, and you

will crave the dark stuff, brewed thick and strong. We chat on the veranda; you like that I have flowers, and potted plants that look well and healthy. I keep house.

'Thank you,' you say, 'for letting me stay.'

I tell you it's nothing, that you're very welcome.

Later, I place a citronella candle in the bathroom before you go in for a shower. I think you like things like that, and you do. This is easy.

The night you come to stay, we attend some literary event and have a lot to drink. I also snort some coke. When I offer it to you, you say no and don't give an explanation. But the alcohol flows thick and fast and deep. Glass after glass of red for me, and dark stout for you straight out of the bottle. Everyone else is drunk too. Including the poet who's been reading from her newly published book that evening. Someone is dancing atop a table. The music is awful and old school, but even this we sway to. You look pretty in your dress and brogues and headband. Once, you place your head on my chest, and close your eyes, and stay there for a long while. Such tenderness. The thing is, at moments like these, I always think it's sweet and rare, and it isn't. It's so easy to feel love. And I know you're hurling yourself into this because you're in a space of great sadness, and what else can I do but allow you to fall so that you're carried elsewhere, wherever that may be. We do not sleep together that

night, but I lie next to you. I don't watch you sleep, but I hold you.

Then we wake in the afternoon and kiss and do not get out of bed.

We do everything else, but I do not fuck you. Yet. Even though you plead, and I like to hear those words fall out of that mouth. *Please. Please.* Then we wash up, and eat, and drink our coffee and tea, and find books to read. You pick up one of mine, and at one point, I glance up to see you looking at me, your hand on a page. You are crying. When I ask you why, you point to a line. It's about a river, and the dead, and how they come down to us when it rains. For a long time, we're both silent. That evening, the day before you leave, we head out for dinner. And who wouldn't think we're together? Except the people at the restaurant have seen me often, with different women by my side, and so they probably don't notice. Always, I sense the heaviness of hope on my arm. Why is everyone always thinking of something more than now?

It's pointless to do so because there's no certainty, from one moment to the next, of what will come. I know. It has happened to me. My wife had said she'd see me later, at dinner, and she didn't. So when you come laden with expectation, I share only so much with you, the bit that arises when plunging into something new. When our bodies are still fresh to each other. There will be nothing more than

this or there will be everything. I refuse to decide. The future happens as it will, as it does.

Then you leave my place like a whisper.

And by the time you return a month later, I've met someone else.

Because life is like that, isn't it? One cannot stop its ebb and flow. You step into the current and whatever's in your path will cross you and touch you and sometimes stay. I don't think too much about what brushes past me. If it happens, it happens. Some sort of belief in organic, even flow, if there's such a thing. You cannot control the weather. You sail where the wind blows.

It is that way.

You return with your suitcase, and a string of shiny fake pearls around your neck, and what else can I do? It's an act of rescue. How can I not? When you are there, all ripe and lovely and so openly mine, I can hardly bear it.

I also think this is convenient. Nothing more. Nothing less.

You're a house guest and I'm being hospitable. I'm showing hospitality in my bed. You're by my side. I'm on you, still not in you.

For that I wait until the next morning, when I know the maid is in the kitchen, and the gardener is outside. And

then I'm in you. I cannot tell you how it's the greatest kind of rush. With you stifling your mouth against my shoulder. I am on top.

In our time together, I don't ask about the one you're married to, because I see this as temporary, of course. What else can it be? Whatever your reasons are, I don't know and I don't question. They are yours. We don't talk about him until much later.

But when we do start talking, I'm surprised by how easy it is.

Maybe because we both write?

That is one reason why this could work out.

And why it won't.

We talk in bed, when the sheets are damp, and the fan whirls above us, endlessly moaning. I confess to cheating. And double, triple timing. You say you've been with married men. I have to admit I haven't told anyone else these things, and neither, you say, have you.

You ask why you cannot be on top.

And I don't tell you. I will, but not now.

I find I talk about my wife more often with you than anyone else. This is disturbing. Sometimes, I feel she is in the same room as us, watching, listening. I haven't had this feeling in years. Why have you brought her back? No, that isn't fair. She was never gone.

Slowly, you talk of the one you married. You say things aren't all right. That there isn't much to salvage. I catch the

word 'companions'. I stay silent. I don't wish to ask, because it might seem as though I'm interested in more. Right now, I'm happy for the current to swirl just as it is. When it changes we will know, and we will adjust. As we always do.

But I do tell you I'm seeing someone else too.

Because it's true. And you've always known about her, and how she's in another city, doing an internship for a few months. At first, I thought this – we, you and I – was a fling thing. Until you mentioned the trouble your marriage was in. But even then. How was I to know?

So this is all the time we have, baby, and somehow, for me that makes it better, more exciting even. It's like the list of ten things you want to do before you die, and actually doing them. We are hedonistic because we have so little time. At first you are cool about this, I think. Also, because we barely mention her. We're too busy fucking.

I'm a teenager again.

It hasn't been this way, ever. So much good sex. And when you lie there, you are a beautiful painting.

We are seen together outside too.

Because we're troublemakers – that's what you call us.

We're performers at heart, you and I. We like to scandalise, to feel rumour flutter around us like starlings. That's why we're good writers, because we know words on paper can elicit the same things. The drama, the spectacle, the mad bid

for immortality. We fall in love with the ones from the Jazz Age. On some nights, our high is as vast as the universe. It is unsustainable. And I love it. We burn, like someone said, at both ends.

From bar to bar. Suddenly, we are everywhere. The parties where there is too much alcohol, and even that isn't enough, so we hunt out the bars that haven't yet closed and drink some more. There are a few we like, and go back to often, without needing to say it to each other. The balcony in a building within some fifteenth-century ruin, that looks out on to a tree lit by lamplight, and beyond that a lake. We like it here because it is both inside and outside. We stand there, Francis and Zelda, endless glasses in hand. Some strangers walk up to us. 'Are you...?' Because I'm old and famous. And I introduce you too, saying this is who you are. And – this is why I love you – you look like you don't care. 'Oh, I must read your book,' the stranger utters politely, and you say, with a swig of your wine, 'In your own time.' I want to kiss you then and there.

Back at home, my place, we smoke pot kept in a plastic muesli jar. Healthy.

You teach me to lace it with coke.

See, behind your Victorian demureness is a streak of madness. We soar and swoop. Upper and downer. It's crazy shit. It hurts our throats; it's sweet in our lungs. We wrestle in the middle, neither high nor low, a lovely purgatory.

Then I tell you that she's coming for a few days on her way to somewhere else.

In other words, I need you to move out.

For a few days. Leave your things here even, and come back as soon as she's gone. I don't think I'll forget the look on your face.

Or your silence.

But what am I to do?

This is all beyond my control.

Although even then, somewhere in my head, I too find it somewhat strange.

And you go with all your things. Apart from a pair of shoes you accidentally leave behind. They are butter yellow, with straps that wrap around your lovely ankles.

In those days, I don't hear from you.

All is quiet.

Except when we bump into each other – you are with friends – at a bar. This city without a river is small, I tell you. She has gone to the loo, and when I turn around, you are there. Looking hurt and tired and small. I'm quite drunk and try to hug you. I don't think you reciprocate. But I continue hugging everyone you're with. Then you all leave. I feel foolish. But a drink takes care of that and everything else.

The next few days, I text but you don't reply.

I persist. Someone once told me I'm like a child. Maybe it's true. After she leaves, I text you furiously. Let's meet, I

insist, let's meet. You finally reply with an abrupt 'OK'. But it's a triumph because I've managed to get you to agree to meet for a drink. Baby, we have only a few more weeks before she returns for good. I haven't told you this, of course; you'll find out as and when it happens. The important thing always is here and now. Didn't someone say that art comes to us proposing frankly to give nothing but the highest quality to our moments as they pass, and simply for those moments' sake? I offer you the same.

This present moment and all its infinite possibilities, and its infinite losses. As soon as it happens, it's gone.

So we meet.

And we come back to my place and we sleep together because it's so good and, fuck, I've missed you in bed, and then you leave.

'Don't be foolish,' I whine. 'Stay, stay, stay.' I repeat that word like a spell, but it fails to charm you. You call for a cab, dress, and go.

In the morning, I text saying, 'When do I see you?'

This time, there isn't much resistance.

There's an art thing you want to attend. Usually, I'm suspicious of these things in this city, unless they come recommended by a few, trusted friends, but I'm eager to please, so I say yes, of course I'll come with you.

I pick you up late afternoon. We drive to the venue. It's a low white building, with neoclassical pillars and a porch,

and large grounds around it, in the heart of the city. You are wearing a blue dress, like something from the '60s, and a floral scarf. You've painted your nails red. You're a sexy stewardess, and I want to take you straight back to bed. But first, art.

And, grudgingly, I admit it's good. A project imagined around the work of a famous sculptor, placed within the building, performed by a theatre troupe in various rooms, and outside. It's multidisciplinary, we're told, and you and I are intrigued. We hold hands, because I don't care who's watching, I never have, and neither do you.

We follow the exhibition trail, and in the lawn we move from site to site, a shifting, moving show. First a tree, and readings from the sculptor's journal about the rain. We listen to his words in the dark. Then we move elsewhere, an amphitheatre, where a group of women cycle around, chatting, on the stage. Their cycles are cherry red. Then a conversation between two men. This goes on for a long time, too long, and you and I are distracted. Finally, thankfully, it ends, and we're taken to the last site. A dance along the skeletal scaffolding on the building's façade. We watch, and then wander to the quiet side, and there we find the red bicycles. We pick one each, hop on; we wobble from years of no practice. Then you hurtle past me, laughing, your dress riding up your thighs. I follow. We go down the path, and then take a right, along the long length of the garden.

I overtake you, and we race, you almost fall, I wait until you steady yourself. The night air is cool and springy and we ride around like sudden children. The performance ends but ours doesn't. People watch us, amused, bewildered. I can tell that you don't want to get off, and neither do I. I could do this forever.

But of course we can't, so we get off, flushed, panting, and put the bicycles away.

We eat dinner, hearty and wholesome, and decide not to order drinks. Then we go home, to my place, and we fall asleep, you, as always, in my arms.

'Why do you hold me through the night?' you ask.

'To keep us safe from ghosts.'

When we lie on the bed, reading, or listening to music, or talking, we must touch. My arm on yours, or our thighs or our feet touching. It's strange. It isn't enough to be in the same room, on the same bed, we must always be in touch.

I can sense you like it. It makes you feel safe.

Soon, we are adopted by a cat, and we name her Dirty Maggi.

Like Thatcher at a strip club.

We feed her tuna out of a can. She likes it and devours it all, then falls asleep on my desk where I write. And you look across at me, from the table where you sit and work, and smile. For a moment, we're like the fucking Holy Family.

Except Dirty Maggi has fleas. So we rush to a pet store and pick up some medicine. 'Just a dab on her collar,' the

storekeeper tells us, but Dirty Maggi is so dirty, we pour the whole thing on her.

She's a beautiful cat, and you love her.

She's striped orange and white and dirt, and has these green eyes, the colour of the first leaves of spring. For hours, she'll sleep, and then she'll leave, as silently as she came.

When she doesn't turn up for a couple of days, you are anxious.

'I hope nothing's happened to her...'

And I tell you she's fine, she's a street cat, shrewd and sharp.

You never seem convinced.

One afternoon, you get very upset.

We are lying on the bed in the guest room. For some reason you've taken a fancy to this place; it's like a cave you say. With the light falling through leaves, from the window. It's a room I hardly use on my own, but with you here, I follow.

I hold my phone before me; we're reading an article someone's posted about an eccentric artist who built himself a museum on an island, when a message comes in.

You belong to me. I belong to you.

You are disconsolate.

I apologise; I do speak to her when you're not around, but this is too blatant, I know.

You are so upset you leave.

I ask if you're coming back later, and I get the cab door slammed in my face.

So in a few hours I follow.

I know the place you've rented. Not far from me. Set back from the ruins and the inside-outside bar where we like to drink. I wait at your door, and you let me in eventually, but don't speak to me. In fact, you move around behaving as though I'm not there.

'Sit, please sit,' I plead.

And you do. Perched on a cushion away from me, like you can't bear to be touched. Somewhere from the other room a song drifts in. '*Setting fire to our insides for fun*'.

When you look at me, I can only see anger and hurt, and once, briefly, hope. That I'll tell you I'm leaving her for you, that there is no one else, only you.

But I'm not that person.

It'll never happen.

Because I've made it clear from the beginning, haven't I?

That there was always somebody else in the picture.

But I cannot bear to lose you even for a short time like this, because I cannot live with loss. It's as though it was all used up when I lost my wife in that accident. A lifetime's capacity for loss taken away overnight. Which is why I just let things be until they run their course, until they shrivel. Because I cannot take the decision to leave, the only choice is to stay.

So I sit there with you, and I do not apologise and I do not promise.

I simply wait until your anger transforms into sorrow.

I can feel it. The air changes in the room.

I suppose this is when I'm meant to 'make up', to offer some gesture towards reconciliation, to try at least to alleviate your sadness.

So I tell you that a friend gave me some opium.

'Let's drink it...'

And without a word, you heat up some water, arrange the glasses, make the tea. I dissolve the deep amber crystals into the steaming liquid. It turns the colour of dark honey. We stir; two prim, proper governesses. We drink at the table, silently. Sip after sip, waiting for the miraculous to wash over us like sleep. The woozy dipping feeling of being in this world and not. The slowing down and sharpening of time. The sense of happiness and nausea. Who says they're not the same thing? After a minute, an hour, you slide into the chair, curling into the cushion. I sit with my insides hurting; my body feeling like it's welded to the couch.

Somehow, I know that after this there won't be much of us. That we will wrestle on a few more beds and part, and come together again. And once I will ask you to dinner, and you will accept, and you will cry into your sake, and when I drop you home I will kiss you, because for that instant I miss you

like a universe. You will look at me with love and hate and something else that I will never be able to place, and then we will drift apart, colliding sometimes in this city's mad bustle. At a café where I'm working on a new manuscript. At a party to celebrate someone else's book launch. At some restaurant or the other, where you are with friends, and I'm with the one who belongs to me. At a winter picnic spread out in the park with ruins around us. And things will mellow. And all this love will turn to friendship tinged forever – no, let's be starkly honest, only for a while – with 'what if'. After that, there will be only accidental meetings, a stray email, a long-lost text. A phone call because you need some advice on a literary project. A quick beer in another city. A thought of each other when something that reminds us of the past catches our eye. Then those too, like everything else, will fade.

For now, though, we lift our glasses and drink.

And fall into delicious stupor, and dream of red bicycles that we ride into the sky.

We race, your dress sliding up your thighs, me in front, and then you. You move swift and strong and steady. And – I'm certain of it – you will leave me behind.

ACKNOWLEDGEMENTS

The good people at HarperCollins India – Ananth Padmanabhan, Udayan Mitra, and Diya Kar Hazra – without whom the book would stand much diminished.

Rahul Soni, for editorial exemplariness and more – fellow movie-list maker, coffee seeker, scaler of forts.

At Borough Press UK, Holly Ainley, my editor by the sea, for connections beyond the pages.

Rashmi Gupta and Bonita Vaz-Shimray, who made the beautiful cover.

My agents, Marina Penalva, Maria Cardona, Leticia Vila-Sanjuán, Anna Soler-Pont, lending raucous support all the way from Spain.

Anuk Arudpragasam, early listener, early encourager on a bright moonlit terrace.

At home, my parents, my sister, uncles, aunts, enthusiastic cheerleaders all.

Away, Paul and Jane Carling, who began every phone conversation with, 'Is it finished?'

Luigi, with whom on an after-ramen stroll in London, the idea for this book came into being.

Oasis, Regina Spektor, Paulo Nutini, Daughter, whose song lines are scattered through this book.

Ashoka University, for time, space, conversations.

Aruni, for inimitable literary advice – 'When you're stuck, throw your character under a bus.'

Tishani, for margarita nights and poetry and the sea.

Jerry, for immense laughter and large-heartedness.

Jeet, who said, 'This sounds good.' It was enough.

Lubs, Koshy, Bora, Gopes, for road trips, and dinners, and other ties that bind.

Sonal, Radhika, work date companions indulgent of our chat-fests and shopping sprees.

Gaurav, for handing me that shovel and walking with me into the forest.

Suraj, for loving trees.

My cat of many names, for happy distraction.

And Pankaj, for being my shelter, my storm.